## She saw it on the dog's collar.

A day grew deep. She touched it, feeling a small circular object. Oh, no. He couldn't have... Her engagement ring.

Daisy opened it, and a ripple of emotion engulfed her. Damn Reid for this visceral reminder of how much she'd loved him.

"Daisy," Reid's voice came from behind, evocative and sensual. "Once upon a time, a boy loved a girl and promised her the world. The girl accepted, returned the promise, and they were to live happily ever after."

Before she could inhale another breath, Reid's hands were on her shoulders. "Nothing has changed, Daisy. I still love you and I still want to give you the world." His arms came around her. "All you have to do is say yes..."

* * *

**The Colorado Fosters:**
They'd do anything for each other...and for love!

# REID'S RUNAWAY BRIDE

BY
TRACY MADISON

Published in Great Britain 2014
by Mills & Boon, an imprint of Harlequin (UK) Limited,
Eton House, 18-24 Paradise Road, Richmond, Surrey, TW9 1SR

© 2014 Tracy Leigh Ritts

ISBN: 978 0 263 91254 8

23-0114

Harlequin (UK) Limited's policy is to use papers that are natural, renewable and recyclable products and made from wood grown in sustainable forests. The logging and manufacturing processes conform to the legal environmental regulations of the country of origin.

Printed and bound in Spain
by Blackprint CPI, Barcelona

**Tracy Madison** lives in northwestern Ohio with her husband, four children, one bear-size dog, one loving-but-paranoid pooch and a couple of snobby cats. Her house is often hectic, noisy and filled to the brim with laugh-out-loud moments. Many of these incidents fire up her imagination to create the interesting, realistic and intrinsically funny characters that live in her stories. Tracy loves to hear from readers. You can reach her at tracy@tracymadison.com.

This story is dedicated to a person who has become very important in my life. Thank you for your kindness, compassion, and seemingly endless support. I am eternally grateful.

## *Prologue*

Less than two hours ago, Daisy Lennox had stood in front of her bedroom windows and breathed in the fragrant scents emanating from her mother's flower garden. The softest of breezes whispered against her cheek with the promise that Steamboat Springs, Colorado, would be blessed with a beautiful spring day. A perfect day, in fact, for a wedding.

For *her* wedding.

She'd closed her eyes and savored the anticipation, as the excitement strummed through her body. By nightfall, she would be Mrs. Reid Foster. It seemed…incredible that this day had finally arrived, that her dreams were so close to becoming reality.

Falling in love with Reid had happened naturally. Effortlessly. He'd been a part of her existence for almost as far back as she could remember, even if it had taken an absurd amount of time for him to view her as anything other than his best friend's little sister.

Once he had, though, neither of them questioned their connection. And when he'd proposed last year, on the evening of her graduation from the University of Colorado, she'd accepted without hesitation. She couldn't imagine her life without him.

With Reid, she felt whole. Reid's love chased off the persistent sensation of not belonging, of not fitting in, of being the odd person out, that she'd battled since childhood.

So, yes. When Daisy had awakened to sunny skies and a warm, fragrant breeze, with hope and delight bubbling in her veins, she had zero reason to believe that anything would—or *could*—interfere with her pure, soul-deep certainty of the future.

Unfortunately, fate had other ideas.

A broken, emotional confession from Daisy's mother had shifted everything she'd ever known to be true into a new reality. This—the story her mother told—was the fodder for bad television, and not the life of a woman who was about to be married.

*None* of this could be real. Yet…somehow, it was.

Emptiness, engulfing and complete, overtook her prior joy. Her breaths came in jagged gasps and her body shook as she attempted to process the unimaginable.

"I know this is a shock," her mother, Clara Lennox, said. She wrapped her arm over Daisy's shoulder and drew her close. "Are you okay?"

*Okay?* No, she was most definitely not okay. She pulled free from her mother's grasp, and as if on their own accord, her fingers reached for the wedding gown she'd laid out on her bed that morning. She crumpled the silky fabric in her fist and tried to bring Reid's face, his voice, his very presence, to mind. Tried to sink herself in his love for her, in hers for him.

"That was a silly thing to ask. Of course you're not okay," Clara said. "How could you be? But…do you think, once this settles some, you'll—"

"Settles? I can't imagine any of this settling in the near future." *Or ever.*

"I understand. I'm sorry for this, sorry for…all of it."

Lifting her chin, Daisy looked at her mother. Her pale

blue eyes were puffy from crying. Her fiery red hair—so like Daisy's own—had been nervously tucked behind her ears while she'd slowly, word by word, shredded the strands of Daisy's identity.

On the morning of her wedding.

"Why today? Why not yesterday or six months ago or when I was ten?" Daisy pushed out the questions, still unable to fully comprehend the magnitude of her mother's confession. "Why would you wait until what is supposed to be the happiest day of my life to tell me that…that—" she swallowed the sobs choking her throat "—I'm not the person I thought I was?"

"You are exactly the same person you have always been." Sighing, Clara ran her hands over her face. "But I shouldn't have waited for so long. I should have—"

"No, Mother. You shouldn't have waited until my wedding day to tell me that I'm the product of an affair!" *Selfish.* Wrong to feel this way, perhaps, but this confession and the timing of it came off as selfish to Daisy. What did this do for her now, other than cause inexplicable amounts of pain and confusion? Not one damn thing. "How could you do this to me?"

"I waited too long," her mother repeated. "I didn't mean to, darling. I just couldn't ever seem to find the right words or the right time or…I kept hoping your father would—"

"Which father?" Daisy's anger rolled in, coating the rest of her spinning emotions. "The man who raised me or the man I didn't even know existed until now?"

Clara reeled back, as if Daisy's words held the physical force of a slap. "Charles Lennox. The man who raised you. The man who accepted you when I admitted my… mistake to him."

"He has never accepted me," Daisy whispered. "And now, I know why."

"You're wrong. He loves you."

"Then why isn't he sitting here with us?"

"Because your father…that is, *we* decided this should come from me."

Not a surprise. If there was one aspect of her father's personality that Daisy understood, it was his reluctance to become embroiled in emotional scenes. Even so, she wished her father had chosen to be here, to offer his support, to give his assurances that he loved her, that he considered her his daughter through and through, and that he always had.

More than a want. She *needed* to hear this.

In that moment, though, with the glorious May sun dappling across her bedroom floor, Daisy didn't fool herself into believing she'd ever hear those assurances from Charles Lennox. If he hadn't been able to do so before, he certainly wouldn't today.

She'd always ached to have the close relationship with her father that her older brother, Parker, did. Over the years, she'd convinced herself that her father simply had more in common with his son than he did with his daughter, and that their relationship, while often distant and cool, had absolutely nothing to do with her. Some men, as her mother consistently said, related better with their male offspring. Some men just weren't able to develop a close connection with their daughters. And this belief, as much as it hurt, had also offered relief.

But this new information, the obvious absence of her father, along with the history of their relationship, painted an altered picture. One that stung in deep and intrinsic ways. She was not Charles Lennox's daughter; she was the product of an affair. What could she possibly mean to him, other than providing the visible proof that his wife had cheated?

In heartbreaking clarity, this understanding answered every question she'd ever had. It explained the distance, the awkward hugs and the lack of pride or enthusiasm whenever Daisy accomplished something. More than anything else, though, this knowledge brought an undeniable logic to her father's unwillingness to…love her the way he loved Parker.

Hell, she wasn't sure she could blame him.

"He isn't even in the house right now, is he?" she asked.

"He…thought we should be alone for this conversation." Clara let out a short breath. "But he said he'll return in time for the wedding."

There was more her mother wasn't saying. The truth of that was written all over her expression, in the tight way she held her body, in the subdued manner in which she spoke. And with sudden, sickening insight, Daisy thought she understood what that something was.

"Oh, my God." Nausea lurched in Daisy's stomach. "After twenty-three years of being my father, he doesn't want to walk me down the aisle, does he? That's why he isn't here. That's why you had to tell me today. He insisted, didn't he?"

"He'll change his mind," Clara said quickly, still not looking at Daisy. "I…hope he'll change his mind once he sees that you won't view him differently now that you know."

"He won't change his mind." This knowledge sat inside Daisy with total certainty, and somehow, the realization was more defeating than the rest. "You know it as well as I do."

Clara faced Daisy. "I *know* he loves you."

"I'm not sure I've ever believed that." Squeezing her eyes shut, Daisy attempted to slow her breathing, to quiet the stirred-up emotions. "Who is my father?"

"Charles Lennox," her mother said stubbornly.

"I wish that were the case." Daisy crumpled the silky fabric of her wedding gown tighter and asked again, "Who is my father?"

Releasing a sigh, Clara said, "What do you want to know?"

"Does he know about me?"

"No. It… We didn't have an actual relationship. Like I said, he was someone I dated in college. I…I knew him before I met Charles, and he was just passing through. Your fath—Charles was out of town so often, and your brother was so little. I was lonely, Daisy. And—" a small sob broke through "—I made a mistake."

That last statement carved into Daisy's heart with the force, the sharpness, of a samurai sword. All she heard was that *she* was the mistake. Not the poor choice her mother made in the heat of the moment, not the one-night stand itself, but that Daisy's very existence was some horrible blunder that could never be corrected.

Unaware of her distress—or, perhaps, just too lost in the past—her mother kept talking, repeating much of what she'd already said. This time, though, Daisy listened to every word, every nuance, every hesitation, and as she did, her sense of self—the person she believed herself to be—slowly and painfully disintegrated. None of what her mother shared eased the agony or the chaos or filled the gaps within. She didn't know who she was. Not really.

"Thank you," she said, interrupting her mother in mid-sentence, having heard enough. "I need to be alone. I need to think. I need to… Just leave for now. Please."

The second that Clara exited the room, Daisy curled up into a ball and allowed her tears free rein. They exploded from deep inside, ravaging through her body with a ferocious intensity. When they stopped, she lay motionless, trying to find meaning in that which held none. Despite how hard she searched, there was nothing to grasp on to for strength, for stability.

Desperate and alone, she thought of Reid and how his love had always given her that strength and stability, a sense of wholeness and security. How just being near him brought all the shady, uneven areas of her life into focus. He made her…real.

And God, she loved him. She did. But the rest of her world had ceased to exist—at least, the world she'd always known, had always believed in—and what remained seemed cloudy and off-balance and without oxygen. She couldn't breathe. Couldn't see the rest of today, let alone tomorrow or the next day or the one after that.

The sudden, frantic need to get away, to find a place she *could* breathe, hit her hard. *No, no, no.* She couldn't do that…couldn't leave Reid and the future she'd craved for so long. How could she do that? He made her real. Who would she be without him?

From the moment they became a couple, she had done everything in her power to show him that she could be exactly the woman he thought she was…the woman he wanted her to be. And unlike with her father, she'd succeeded with Reid. She didn't have to fight so hard to gain his acceptance, his affection or his approval.

Really, all she had done was follow the path he'd created, whatever that path was, whether that meant her— *their*—choice of colleges, the timing of their engagement, their wedding date, even the details of their wedding. Reid made everything, from the smallest hurdle to the largest, easy. He knew what he wanted, and Daisy loved him, so she wanted what he did.

Didn't she? Of course she did. Of course.

Another series of breathless sobs broke free. She wrapped her arms around her legs, pulling them closer to her chest. With Reid, she would always know who she was, where she belonged. She would never have to guess or struggle…or…

Oh, Lord. No. Just…no.

One by one, memories jabbed into her consciousness,

forcing her to confront the impossible. Throughout her life, she had attempted to become the daughter she believed Charles Lennox wanted. She'd formed her decisions, her interests, around him. And she had done so for the specific purpose of creating a loving relationship with her father.

Now she understood why she had continually failed. But with Reid, she hadn't failed. They were to be married that very afternoon. In front of family and friends, but without her father by her side. In a wedding ceremony that Reid had planned from beginning to end, without Daisy uttering one word of complaint or offering her opinion.

She would simply sit back, nod and smile. Happy to do whatever he wanted, however he wanted. Not his fault, she knew, but hers. He was, for all intents and purposes, a force of nature. She had grabbed on to his energy, his strength of will, and let the tide carry her.

By doing so, she had become the woman Reid Foster professed to love, and with that love came definition. An identity. She was *his* girlfriend, *his* fiancée, now…soon, *his* wife. Maybe in a year or two or three, the mother of his children.

Who would she be if she hadn't muted herself for her father, for Reid? Would Reid even love her if she hadn't morphed into the woman she believed he wanted?

An unrelenting pressure stole the air from Daisy's lungs, shuddered through her and stifled her sobs. She didn't know the answer to either of those questions. Didn't know if Reid would still want her, love her, and she couldn't see a version of herself that didn't include Reid.

*He makes me real.*

But…shouldn't she be real on her own? Shouldn't she know who she was, regardless if Charles Lennox were her father or not? Regardless if she were Reid's wife or not?

Shouldn't she be able to find some type of strength and security and confidence within herself?

The answer was swift and tragic and…honest. *Yes.*

Sitting up, Daisy stared at her wedding gown, unable to believe that she was on the cusp of making such an unbearable, heart-wrenching decision. But she was. She had.

Fresh tears filled her eyes. Oh, God…she had.

She wiped her cheeks, took in a fortifying breath, and the soothing stillness of calm certainty took control. Yes. She had made her decision. There would not be a wedding today.

Daisy reached for the phone, her intent to call Reid and have him come over. So she could explain the horrifying details of what she'd learned, of her decision and the reasons for it, the best she could, face-to-face. He deserved nothing less. She *knew* this.

In the end, she just couldn't do it. Seeing him now, when her emotions were so raw, when she felt lonelier than she ever had in her life, would do her in. She wouldn't cancel the wedding or leave Steamboat Springs. She wouldn't be able to say goodbye.

Reid's commanding presence, his love for her, his absolute surety that they belonged together, would convince her to ignore what her instincts were all but shouting. Far easier and less painful to follow in his wake and become his wife, than to trust her newfound convictions and…leave. Start over. Become real on her own, without her family. Without…Reid.

Even as she wrote the letter, even as she carefully folded the tearstained pages and removed her engagement ring, even as she packed her suitcase, and even as she quietly slipped out of the house she'd grown up in, she kept waiting for something—an inner voice, a sign, *anything*—to change her mind. To stop her from leaving the man she loved.

Nothing did.

Dear Reid,

This morning, my life shattered into a million unrec-
ognizable pieces. As it turns out, my father is not my
father, and therefore, he is unwilling to walk me down
the aisle. And I don't know if you can understand this,
but this information has made me feel lost, without
balance, and I need to figure out how to fix this.

I can't believe, even now, that I have made this decision or that it feels so right. But I have, and it does.
I'm sorry I don't have the strength or the courage to
tell you this in person, but I have to leave. This is
about me, not you. I know that sounds clichéd and
awful. In this case, though, it's the complete truth.

My love for you hasn't disappeared. I doubt my
love for you will ever disappear, and even as I write
this, I still want to marry you…. Just not today.
Maybe, if fate is on our side and you can find it within
yourself to forgive me, we'll have another chance in
the future. A second chance at forever.

Someday.

Please, please forgive me.


All my love,
Daisy

# Chapter One

Snowflakes, plump as a cherub's cheeks, spewed and spat in the wind-soaked air, where they whirled in a mad, frenetic dance before they dropped to the ground and coated the world—this part of the world, anyway—in a thick, icy canopy of pure white.

Why *wouldn't* Steamboat Springs, Colorado, be in the middle of a roaring winter storm on the night of the runaway bride's return? Nothing else would've made any sense.

Gritting her teeth in concentration, Daisy attempted to see through the blinding snow as she navigated the last several miles to her brother's house. Truth be told, she should've stayed overnight in Grand Junction when she heard the weather report. She hadn't for the simple reason that she'd wanted to complete the last leg of her journey without delay.

She'd left her home in Los Angeles at the crack of dawn, and barring the intermittent stops to walk her dog, had made excellent time. Another four hours of driving—even with a winter storm warning in place—had seemed preferable to putting off the inevitable for another day. So, with the hope that she'd beat the worst of the storm, she'd pushed onward.

Well, four hours had turned into six-plus hours, and if what brewed outside her car wasn't the worst of the storm, then Daisy figured it was soon to come. Her only goal at this point was to be safely ensconced inside Parker's home when that moment arrived.

Sighing, she slid to a halt at a stop sign and tried to set aside the ridiculous notion that this storm was Mother Nature's way of warning her off, of reminding Daisy that she wouldn't be welcomed in her hometown after close to an eight-year absence.

And really, the thought *was* absurd.

It was the end of February, for crying out loud, so snowstorms in Colorado were far from unheard of. They were, in fact, more the norm than not. This bit of logic, however, didn't stop the anxiety from roiling in her stomach. Gripping the steering wheel tighter, she made a careful right-hand turn, just as the GPS instructed. How many folks would even remember her name, let alone her hotfooted retreat from the wedding altar and the man she was supposed to marry?

Couldn't be too many, she assured herself. Out of those who happened to remember both Daisy and the details of that long-ago May morning? The majority of that group would likely be a great deal more curious about her reappearance than they would be unwelcoming.

Unfortunately, she knew what rested at the center of her unease, and it wasn't the weather or the general population of Steamboat Springs. Nope, the reason for her pumped-up nerves and racing heart could be found in one man and one man only: Reid Foster.

The man she'd left behind.

Just the thought of seeing Reid again brought forth a slew of shivers and complicated, complex emotions. They hadn't spoken even once since the day she'd ended their relationship and had discarded their future in favor of a quickly packed suitcase and a bus out of town.

She'd wanted to. Had damn well yearned to speak with him, to fully explain why she'd behaved so cowardly and left him with a letter, instead of an honest conversation. Months had passed before she gathered enough courage to call.

When she finally did, Parker had answered Reid's phone. Unexpected, as Parker had lived in Boston then, but also—due to her brother's friendship with Reid—not terribly surprising. And he'd stated that she'd caused enough damage. That the best thing she could do for everyone was to leave well enough alone and forget about Reid.

If her brother had been unkind, she might not have listened. But in truth, he'd sounded sad and serious, rather than rude and blaming. She heard his deep concern, and in a flood of self-awareness, Daisy had understood—completely—the pain she'd caused.

So, because Parker's stance made sense and the last thing she wanted was to create any additional pain, she chose to live with her guilt and heed his advice. Good advice, as it turned out, since Reid hadn't attempted to contact her in all of these years, either.

But now, by the sole virtue of being back in Steamboat Springs, they'd bump into each other eventually. If not in some strange, random occurrence—such as at the grocery store—then either at the hospital, where Parker was recovering from a serious skiing accident, or at the house, where Daisy would be caring for her two young nieces, Erin and Megan, in the interim.

Regardless of the specifics, Daisy felt sure she'd find Reid in her line of vision sooner rather than later. Fate would demand nothing less. And she couldn't imagine what that scene would look like, sound like, feel like. And that meant she couldn't prepare.

Strange, really, how in some ways, the past eight years seemed as if an entire lifetime had elapsed, but in other ways, those exact same years were no more than a few seconds of a ticking clock. Or, perhaps more accurate in this scenario, a ticking bomb.

Over those years, she'd created a life. Had made friends and figured out how to work for herself, and now made a decent living. She'd even found her biological father, had spent a little time getting to know him, only to realize that he did not hold any answers for her. Only she could provide those. And, for the most part, she had.

She understood who she was. How she needed to live in order to survive, to remain true to herself, and seeing Reid again could potentially undo all of that.

So, yes, a ticking bomb was a fair and accurate comparison.

A strong gust of wind yanked the car to the side, catapulting Daisy to renewed awareness of her surroundings. Muttering a curse, she eased off the gas pedal and breathed in relief when the car returned to the road. None of what might or might not happen in the coming days mattered right now. All that did was getting off the road and to her brother's house.

Parker hadn't phoned her until almost a full week after his accident. Again, not unexpected. Her relationship with her entire family had remained distant and uncomfortable. If anything, she was surprised to be notified at all. By anyone.

But he'd been half-loopy from pain medications, and it had taken a while for Daisy to understand how serious his injuries were. Learning how close he had come to dying scared her, had made her realize how much time they had wasted. She'd already decided to return to her hometown when Parker asked if she would look after his daughters while he recovered.

Her sister-in-law—Parker's wife, Bridget—had died three years earlier from cancer, and Daisy and Parker's parents now lived in Florida. She had no doubt that if Charles Lennox weren't recovering from hip-replacement surgery, it would be her parents caring for the girls. So she supposed she was the obvious choice, but she'd still been surprised by Parker's request.

Naturally, she'd said yes.

But she hadn't considered that she barely knew her nieces, having only met them twice before. Once when Parker had brought his family to California, and then, at his wife's funeral in Boston, where the couple had met and made their home. Just short of a year after becoming a widower, Parker had returned to Steamboat Springs to raise his daughters.

And, other than the customary phone calls on birthdays and holidays, Daisy and Parker rarely spoke. So, no. She didn't know her nieces. She didn't know their likes or dislikes, what made them happy or sad, or any of the other myriad details that made up their lives.

A new rush of fear hit Daisy. How was she supposed to provide the security her nieces were sure to need when she'd spent so little time with them?

One way or another, she'd have to figure it out.

She also hadn't thought about what it would be like to breathe in the same air as Reid Foster, to look into his sinfully dark eyes or to listen to the slow, deep, evocative cadence of his voice again after so freaking long. Any of those occurences might prove to be her undoing.

"Everything will be fine," she said, forcing firmness into her tone. "Parker will make a full recovery. The girls and I will get to know each other. I'm their aunt, so they'll love me. Of course they will! And seeing Reid again won't be easy, but I'll survive."

Her dog, a rescue whippet whose brindle coat held varying shades of white, fawn and gray, whined plaintively from the backseat in a definite plea to get out of the car.

"Soon, Jinx," Daisy said in a soothing voice. "We're almost there."

Due to her shock at Parker's accident and her hurried departure, Daisy had forgotten to mention that she was bringing Jinx with her. Hopefully, neither of the girls was afraid of dogs, because she refused to kennel Jinx for however long her stay might last.

Whippets—a medium-size breed that originated from greyhounds—were intensely devoted to their owners, and since Jinx was a rescue dog, building the trust between them had taken close to six months. Not bringing her along was out of the question.

The GPS announced that Daisy had arrived at her destination. Slowing to a crawl, she located the proper house and parked the car as close to the side of the road as she could. She pulled in a fortifying breath and gave herself a few minutes to gather her bearings while staring at her brother's home. Between the darkness and the blowing snow, she couldn't see much, but the outside light was on, casting a friendly glow. A safe haven.

For now, at least.

Parker had stated that a few of his neighbors were pitching in until Daisy could take over, so she guessed the girls were safely tucked in for the night at one of the other houses dotting the street. She'd see them tomorrow. Her brother had also promised to have someone leave a key under the porch mat, so Daisy would have access to the house. She prayed he hadn't overlooked this not-so-small detail, otherwise, she'd be back on the road, searching for shelter.

"Well, Jinx," she said. "I guess we're here."

And, because there was nothing left to do other than go inside, Daisy leashed and picked up her dog, grabbed her overnight bag—the rest of her luggage could wait until morning—and pushed her way through the whipping snow toward the welcoming light.

"Ready or not," she whispered into the howling wind, "here I come."

Exhaustion, pure and complete, seeped through Reid Foster's body. He leaned against the wall in the Lennoxes' upstairs hallway, let out a bone-weary sigh and hoped the girls were as sound asleep as they'd appeared. The prior week and a half had taught him that one or the other—sometimes both—would fall victim to unquenchable thirst within minutes of their bedroom light going out. Sometimes, they just wanted another hug.

Either way, he figured he'd wait right here for a bit. Just in case.

Erin and Megan were scared, and rightly so. They'd already lost their mother, had already learned that even parents can get hurt, or sick, and go away forever. His heart wouldn't allow him to do anything other than care for them the best he could. Most days, that meant rushing from work to pick them up and bring them home, so they could exist in familiar surroundings, with their toys and their own beds to sleep in.

But Lord, he was tired.

During the winter months, his job as a ski patroller often demanded extended hours filled with physically draining, challenging work. Toss in the care and well-being of two frightened children, along with visiting Parker whenever he could, and Reid was running fairly scarce on energy. Especially tonight.

With forewarning of the storm, which was now raging outside, and completing the necessary preparations, work had started early and ended late. When he'd arrived at the next-door neighbor's house to collect the girls, he noticed they were more high-strung than normal. Soon enough,

Reid discovered that they'd watched some tearjerker of a family movie about several children who were unexpectedly orphaned.

The neighbor had clued in to Reid's disapproval and had apologized, stating she hadn't realized the plot of the movie until the girls were engrossed. At that point, she felt she would've done more damage by not allowing them to finish watching it. Reid didn't know about that, but the next hour of the evening had then been filled with one question after another.

Seven-year-old Erin, the elder of the two, who looked to be growing into a near replica of her aunt Daisy—both in personality and, other than the color of her eyes, appearance—had asked who would take care of her and Megan if their daddy died like their mommy had?

Initially, Reid was at a loss. Honesty, he decided, was the best route, so he'd—once again—explained that all indications stated that Parker was out of danger and on the road to a full recovery. And he was, though from what Reid understood, Parker had another surgery facing him, followed by months of physical therapy.

Five-year-old Megan hadn't said a word, just sat there and watched Reid with her sad, fearful brown eyes. She'd looked so lonely that he'd picked her up and put her on his lap, where she snuggled against his chest and gripped his shirtsleeve as if it were a life preserver.

Refusing to let the rest of her question go, Erin had jutted out her chin—a mannerism that, again, had Daisy written all over it—and asked, "But if something happened to Daddy, who would take care of us? I don't want to be in a f-foster home."

*Damn that movie.* "Sweet pea, that would never happen," Reid had said, and he'd meant it, but the truth was that he had no idea what Parker's plans were if such a cri-

sis ever occurred. He could, however, guess at the likeli-
est candidates.

He started with Parker's parents, Charles and Clara Lennox, who had retired to Florida several years earlier, and
then moved on to the girls' maternal grandparents, who
lived in Boston. While he knew Erin and Megan had a good
relationship with both sets of their grandparents, neither
answer fully satisfied the elder Lennox daughter.

With a quietly contemplative expression, she'd asked,
"What if they can't? Who then?"

Reid had fumbled for a second before naming their aunt
Daisy, not fully believing that Parker would trust the care
of his daughters to someone who was a virtual stranger, but
unable to latch on to another person that would make sense.

Saying Daisy's name aloud—something he rarely did—
caused him a fleeting spasm of pain, of loss…a little bewil-
derment, along with a good, solid dose of anger.

At Daisy, for not giving them a chance before taking off.
At himself, too, for keeping silent on the very same news
that had sent her running. He should've told her the truth
about her paternity when he learned of it, and not decided
to wait until after they were married.

Perhaps if he had, she would've leaned on him, trusted
in him and their relationship, instead of bolting and never
looking back. To this day, she had no idea that he could
have saved her from her mother's ill-timed confession. No
one, not even Parker, knew about the argument he'd overheard between Clara and Charles Lennox the week before
the wedding.

That was a secret he still kept.

So, yeah, he'd kicked himself over his misguided actions. But he couldn't undo them. And Daisy had made the
decision to leave him and their future without so much as
a conversation. In his estimation, that made both of them
wrong and neither of them blameless.

But Reid was a practical man, and as the years had piled up on one another, he'd learned to keep the past where it belonged. Mostly, this mindset had proven successful.

Mostly wasn't always, though, so mentioning Daisy as a possible guardian for the girls evoked the same mixed bag of reactions he'd become resigned to dealing with. As usual—at least for the last long while—those feelings dissipated as abruptly as they'd appeared, and Reid had returned his focus to the little girl on his lap and the one standing directly in front of him.

"Listen to me, angel," he'd said, purposely speaking in a slow and authoritative voice. "I will never let you live in a foster home. I will always be here for you and your sister."

Erin's pinched expression softened slightly. "Do you promise?"

"I promise."

That had done the trick, and shortly, the three were crowded around the tiny table in the girls' bedroom, having a tea party with their favorite stuffed animals. After which, he'd prepared dinner, and the rest of the evening had flown by with various activities. The highlight, of course, was speaking with their father, and the promise that they should be able to visit him soon.

Baths and tickling and bedtime stories—three of them—followed. Both girls had seemingly drifted off toward the end of the last, and Reid had tucked them in, kissed them on their cheeks and gone into the hallway to stand guard.

Deciding enough time had passed to believe they were good and truly out, Reid pushed himself off the wall and yawned. He'd straighten the kitchen, since he hadn't after dinner, shower and see if he could stay awake long enough to catch the news. Or…hell, maybe he'd skip all of it and just hit the sack, try to get up early enough to—

Muffled sounds that couldn't be what he thought drifted up the stairs from the living room. A barking dog? *In* the house? Had one of the girls turned on the television when he hadn't noticed? Had to be that, because he remembered locking the front door. Still, he took the stairs two at a time, and when he reached the landing, every damn hair on his arms stood up straight.

He didn't need to take another step to recognize the low, sultry voice emanating from around the corner. It didn't matter how many years had passed, that voice had been branded into his brain for all eternity. Without a doubt, Daisy Lennox—the woman he'd once envisioned spending the rest of his life with—had come home.

Dumbfounded, Reid froze and…just listened. She crooned to what he assumed was the dog he'd heard, saying something about kibble and a fresh bowl of water. One by one, each of his senses went on high alert, and his earlier mixed bag of emotions returned with a bang.

Part of him wanted to walk into the living room, pull her into his arms and take up where they'd left off—no questions asked. The other part wanted to go upstairs and hightail it out of a bedroom window, just so he'd never again have to look her in the eyes.

The first idea was foolhardy and beyond ludicrous. The second was gutless and as impossible as the first. Even if behaving cowardly were in Reid's DNA, he wouldn't sneak off while the girls were sleeping. He wouldn't disappear on them, now or ever. With or without a letter.

To Reid's way of thinking, that left him with a solitary option: man up and announce his presence, remain polite and calmly let Daisy know—since he had to assume her arrival was due to learning of Parker's accident—that he had everything under control.

Shouldn't take much to get her to leave, and this time, he'd be relieved—hell, happy—to send her on her way. Right. She'd be gone within two days. Certainly no more than three.

He could keep the peace for three days, couldn't he? Yup, that he could. Decision made, Reid relaxed his features into an emotionless mask and forced his leaden legs to carry him forward. As he walked, he focused on three words: *calm, polite* and *detached.*

Of course, those three words evaporated the second he rounded the corner into the archway that separated the house's entrance from the living room, the second his eyes settled on the woman he'd never been able to forget. She was still beautiful. Still…Daisy.

Seeing him, she gasped, but didn't speak. Neither did he.

At some juncture, she'd cut her long, coppery red hair into a short, wispy style that pulled attention to her arresting green-blue eyes and the delicate angles of her face. She was dressed inappropriately for February in Colorado, wearing a lightweight jacket over what appeared to be a summery dress and a pair of…clogs? Yeah, clogs. The woman was insane.

But achingly familiar. The Daisy he'd fallen for had lived in her own head, her own secret world, and had rarely taken notice of anything as practical as the weather. It seemed that some things, regardless of time, hadn't changed.

Reid's breath locked in his lungs as the past crept up and swarmed him with memories. In a split second, he was reliving the worst moment of his life, the moment he'd read that damn letter of hers and the sickening, unbelievable realization that she'd left. The anger, the sadness, the self-recriminations and wondering if he had behaved differently, if she would have, as well.

All of it was there, fresh and alive and…potent. The years spanning those many yesterdays with today vanished, and Reid forgot about remaining polite, calm and detached.

"Hello, darlin'," he drawled, ignoring the crazy rat-a-tat beat of his heart. "By my calculations, you're…oh, about seven years and nine months late for our wedding."

## Chapter Two

"I can do better." Daisy kept her voice smooth and without inflection. Fate, it seemed, had decided not to waste a second in putting Reid Foster in her line of vision. "Seven years, nine months and four days. I can probably figure out the hours and minutes, if you'd like."

"Nah." Leveraging his right shoulder against the inner-archway wall, Reid angled his arms across his chest in a laid-back, nonchalant manner. Irritating that he seemed so at ease when Daisy had yet to catch her breath. "The broad strokes are more than sufficient."

Her brain tried to process a reply, but failed. How in heaven's name was she supposed to have a conversation with this man at this moment? Impossible. She couldn't think.

Somewhat regrettably, she also couldn't stop staring.

Naturally, he looked good. She wouldn't have expected anything less. He wore dark denim and a thick flannel shirt in shades of soft greens and dark blues. He had the same coal-black hair cropped close to his head, the same strong, lithely muscular form and the same ingrained power that all but sprang from every pore of his body.

The same Reid. Yet…not exactly. There was an aura of

toughness—a hardness, she supposed—that hadn't existed in *her* Reid. Had she done that to him? Maybe. Probably.

Guilt layered in, joining the already complex synthesis of her emotions, tying her tongue into knots and making her wish—desperately—that she'd stayed overnight in Grand Junction.

"I…um…didn't expect to find anyone here." One memory after another clicked into being. *Breathe. All I have to do is breathe.* "I expected the girls to be at a neighbor's house."

"They're at the neighbor's when I'm working," Reid said, maintaining his casual persona, as if seeing her again held zero effect. Lucky him. "Otherwise, they're with me."

*Of course.* Why hadn't she considered that Reid would be helping with Erin and Megan? She should have. He remained close friends with Daisy's brother, and the Reid she remembered had always been there for the people he cared about.

"That's…nice of you," she said, infusing brightness into her tone. "I'm here now to take up the slack. Exhausted after the long drive, but here."

An indefinable emotion darkened Reid's gaze. He appraised her quietly, his body tense, his jaw hard. "So… you're here to take up the slack, are you?"

"That's right." Reid continued to stare at her in that silent, steady way of his. To combat the silence and the stare, she pushed out the first words that entered her head. "How's life been treating you? I mean…um…are you doing well?"

"Oh, I'm friggin' fantastic," Reid muttered. "Life's a dream."

"That's really great to hear, and—"

"What about you, Daisy? How have you been since I saw you last…when was that, exactly?" Pausing, as if in deep reflection, Reid suddenly smiled and winked. "I got it. The last time I saw you was at our rehearsal dinner, correct? The night before you took off."

There it was, out in the open. "Yes, that would be correct," she said, matching his sarcasm, note for note. "I've been wonderful! Thanks so much for asking."

Heavy silence hung between them, layering the air with unsaid words and questions. All of which had to do with their past, with the decision Daisy had made on that long-ago day. And okay, she owed Reid what she hadn't been able to give him then, but having that particular discussion now seemed inappropriate and rushed and…far too painful.

Right or wrong, fair or unfair, she just wasn't ready.

Thankfully, Jinx decided the quiet was her opportunity to make herself known. She whined and tugged at the leash. While she only stood about twenty inches tall and weighed twenty-four pounds, she could be quite determined when she set her mind to it.

Relieved to have a millisecond to reel in her shock, Daisy unhooked the leash from the dog's collar. "There you go, sweets," she said to Jinx. "Explore to your heart's content."

Without delay, Jinx began to sniff the hardwood floor and whatever objects she came àcross. Daisy watched for a few minutes, using the break to gather her strength, her balance. And while she watched, she took in her surroundings.

Awash in vivid colors, the living room held a bright red sofa that stretched in front of a bay window, on which were a plethora of handicrafts likely created by her nieces. Next to the couch sat a sunny yellow chair that was large enough to hold two adults—or, Daisy imagined, a father and his young daughters—and had more in common with a puffy cloud than an actual piece of furniture. She could live in a chair like that.

Rounding out the room was a television, a pair of squat bookshelves filled with an array of children's books and a square, low-to-the-ground coffee table that was perfect for game nights, crafts or eating a meal while watching a favorite TV show or movie.

A comfortable place, filled with energy and life. Daisy could easily envision two little girls playing and laughing and growing up here. Somehow, that thought boosted her resolve.

She was here for a reason. A reason that had zip to do with Reid Foster.

And right now, even standing in the same room with him had annihilated her equilibrium. Therefore, her first order of business was claiming her brother's home as her territory.

Before she could proceed, Jinx's low, rumbling growl met Daisy's ears. A quick bolt of untimely humor cut into her anxiety. Biting the inside of her lip to stop the grin from emerging, she stood and pivoted so that she faced Reid. Yep, just as she'd thought.

Jinx's teeth were embedded in the cuff of Reid's jeans and, with her body buckled in concentration, her dog was valiantly attempting to tug him to the door and out of the house. While whippets were highly energetic dogs, most tended to be quiet with sweet and loving temperaments. When it came to men, however, Jinx defied the typical.

She flat-out disliked men. *All* men.

The rescue service through which Daisy had adopted Jinx hadn't been able to provide a specific reason as to why, though they had warned Daisy of the oddity early on in the process. Even after months of becoming acquainted with her few male friends, Jinx hadn't warmed up in the slightest. So, no, Daisy wasn't surprised by Jinx's behavior.

She was, however, highly amused by the dog's timing.

"Jinx!" Daisy said, hiding her laughter. "Stop beating up on the poor man."

The dog didn't hesitate. If anything, her tugging grew more exuberant, more purposeful. Enough so, that Reid had to give up his kicked-back pose in order to sustain his balance.

Standing straight, he glanced from Jinx to Daisy. "Dare I ask?"

"Don't take it personally," Daisy said, biting her lip harder. "She isn't a fan of men. And while she's very well-behaved in other areas, she…tends to ignore me when a man is around."

"You have a man-hating dog?" Reid gently jiggled his leg in a failed attempt to unhinge Jinx's teeth. "Did she come that way or did you train her?"

"Trained her, of course," Daisy said with a straight face. "After all, a single woman living in L.A. has to have some type of defense in today's world."

Reid's lips quirked in the beginnings of a smile, causing the rigid line of his jaw to relax a miniscule amount. Maybe Jinx had broken the ice. It was a nice, if overly hopeful, thought.

"I don't know," he said. "If protection was your goal, you might have considered choosing a larger, more menacing breed of dog."

"Oh, she does the job well enough. She has you good and cornered, doesn't she?"

"I'm humoring her," Reid said, his tone sandpaper-dry. "Until she loses interest."

"She's stubborn on this account."

"I'm fairly sure I can outwait a dog."

"You can try, but as long as you're here, she won't stop." Deciding to make her stance clear before the energy in the room shifted again, Daisy pulled every ounce of her strength to the surface and said, "Just be careful when you leave that you don't let Jinx out. She runs like the wind, and I don't relish the idea of chasing her down in this snow."

"Good to know." Reid shook his leg harder. All that did

was compel Jinx to grab on tighter, growl louder and pull with increased force. "But I'm not going anywhere."

"Um…of course you are," Daisy said firmly. "You're going home."

Dark, molasses-hued eyes met hers in a silent challenge. "Why would I do that?"

"Simple. I'm here now."

He looked at her with incredulity. Maybe with the slightest touch of annoyance, as well. "This isn't that simple, Daisy. Not by any stretch of the imagination."

"I disagree." On the basics, anyway, if not the complete picture. "The girls don't need two caregivers, and since I'm here, there isn't any reason for you to stay."

"There are plenty of reasons," he countered, his voice growing cooler with each syllable. "I've been here the entire time. You have not. The girls know me. They do not know you. Add in the difficulty of what they're going through, how scared they are about their father, and the last thing they need is for anything else to change in their worlds."

Valid points, all of them. And damn it, she even agreed with his take. Because no, she didn't want to upset her nieces or add yet another degree of turmoil into their lives. But she absolutely didn't want Reid here mucking with her emotions.

"I admit I haven't spent much time with Erin and Megan, but we talk on the phone every now and again, and I send them gifts throughout the year," Daisy said, forcing authority into her voice, her demeanor. "I am not a stranger to them."

"Not being a stranger is a hell of a lot different than knowing someone enough to feel comfortable or safe." Reid swore again, this time under his breath. Whether at the still frantic Jinx or at Daisy's statement, she couldn't speculate. Probably both. "And let's face the facts here. You don't know them any better than they know you."

Hurt by his words, by the truth of them, Daisy removed her wet coat and kicked off her shoes. No, she didn't know her nieces, and she hated that it had taken something as horrible as her brother's accident to propel her to change the status quo. But she was here now.

"That doesn't mean we won't get to know each other, or that they won't eventually become comfortable. I'm their family, Reid."

"Family? Depends on your definition. Mine has to do with being present, available, for the people you love." Reid gave his leg another jerk, this one somewhat stronger than the last. Jinx, bless her heart, held on tight. "I'm not entirely sure my definition applies here."

Wow. Just…wow. The need to offer a defense came on strong, but why bother? Yes, she'd kept her distance from her family, but Parker and her parents had done the same with her. The culpability—in this regard, anyway—did not wholly rest on her shoulders. More to the point, she didn't owe Reid any explanations on this aspect of her life. Not a one.

"Seeing how I'm standing in my brother's home right this very instant, I'm fairly sure your definition does apply," she said, managing to hold her temper in check. "I don't know what your expectations are, but—"

"My expectations," Reid said, slowing his words to a crawl, "are that you'll visit with your brother, assure yourself of his health and future prognosis, spend a little time with your nieces and go back home. That will take two, maybe three days. Four on the outside."

"Hold on here. Are you asking me to leave?" Daisy took one step forward, stopped and planted her hands on her hips. "Or are you *ordering* me to leave?"

"Neither." His shoulders tensed in frustration. "And my goal isn't to sound rude, but no one here is counting on you, Daisy. There isn't any need for *you* to hang around."

*Ouch.* "Guess what, Reid? You don't get to shoo me off as if I'm some pesky bug." Sudden moisture dotted her eyes, threatening tears. "And in case you're wondering, Parker asked me to come, so I'd say *he* is counting on me."

"Parker—" Shaking his head in disbelief, Reid said, "I can't fathom a reasonable scenario where your brother would ask for your help. He knows I have everything under control."

"Of course you have everything under control, that's your mantra, isn't it?" *Whoa.* Unfair in this circumstance. Unfair, Daisy admitted, in *any* circumstance. Reid—his current level of rudeness notwithstanding—had never pushed for control, he'd just…stepped into the role with ease. "That was uncalled for and I apologize. But this is not about us."

"Nope, this isn't about us." Reid gave Jinx—who hadn't yet relented in her growl-and-tug approach—an exasperated, are-you-kidding-me-just-stop-already sort of scowl. "This is about Erin and Megan and what is best for them."

"Which is what I just said!"

"Not really, no." Now his eyes were flat, almost…cold. "You state that I should leave, without asking one question about the well-being of your nieces. What's going on with them, how they're doing, if there is anything you should know before you give their primary caregiver a boot out the door. Tell me, how is any of that what's best for Erin and Megan?"

"I'm their aunt, whether you like that fact or not." She counted to three, then to five. Unfortunately, her frustration didn't subside. It grew larger. "Parker asked for my help," she repeated. "I'm here for my brother and my nieces, and I don't want—"

"Put yourself in their place, if you can," he said, interrupting Daisy. "Try to imagine how they would feel to wake up in the morning and find you here and me gone.

Without any warning or explanation." Reid snapped his fingers. "Just gone."

She stifled a gasp as Reid's full inference hit home. He wasn't only speaking of Erin and Megan's feelings, but a reflection of his own from when he read her goodbye letter. Traversing that pothole-ridden road now wouldn't solve anything, though. Not when their emotions, their shock at seeing one another again, remained so high.

Better, easier, to focus on the issue of who would stay to watch the girls and who would leave. And, at the end of the day, only one person had the authority to send Daisy packing. That person, no matter how much he might wish it to be so, was not Reid.

Lifting her chin, she said, "I'm not going anywhere. I'm staying for the duration, however long that might last. Unless Parker says different."

"Is that so?"

"That's so." She raised her chin another notch. "You'll have to find a way to deal with my being here, because that is not changing. I'm taking over the girls' care from here on out."

"Oh, I can deal. But, sweetheart—" Jinx's antics finally proved too much. Bending at the waist, Reid disengaged the dog from his jeans, swept her into his arms and muttered, "Behave." To Daisy, he said, "You are not taking over and I am most certainly not leaving."

"We both can't stay. That would mean…"

"That's right. As of now, we're living together." Reid's long legs ate up the space between them in mere seconds. Passing Jinx from his arms into hers, he said, "This will be cozy, don't you think? Why, we'll almost be like one big, happy family."

*Oh, hell, no.* "You're crazy. That won't work."

"Trust me, I'm not overly fond of the idea, but there isn't another viable option."

"You leave. I stay. There, problem solved."

"Sure. If you can answer three questions about Erin and Megan, I'll pack up and leave tonight. We'll even start with a simple one," he said. "What are their favorite colors?"

Ten…twenty…thirty seconds ticked by. Pink? Probably for one of them, if not both. Purple, maybe. But she didn't want to guess. She wanted to *know*.

Swallowing, she gave a short nod of concession. "Point made. But I don't see how this… We can't just…" Daisy searched for another solution. Just one. And came up lacking. "Supposing I agree, how long will this living-together thing last?"

"No clue. Later, once the three of you are better acquainted, we can reassess. For now, as much as I hate to admit it—" he looked upward, as if praying for divine intervention "—we're in this together. Lock, stock and barrel."

Damn it. Damn *him*. He was right.

Here she was, almost eight years later, being pulled along by the force of Reid Foster. She had no defense against his bulletproof logic. Nothing she could do or say to get out of this ridiculous situation. Other than turn around and get back in her car and return home.

And she couldn't—wouldn't—do that. "Fine," she said stiffly. "We can discuss the details tomorrow. I'm exhausted. Is there a guest room I can use?"

Her agreement eased the lines of tension creasing Reid's forehead. Stroking his jaw as if in thought, he said, "Good question. There are only two bedrooms. The girls share one, and the other is Parker's. I've been bunking there. And I'd be happy to sleep on the sofa, but…"

"But…?"

"The girls sometimes drift in at night if they've had a bad dream, or if they wake in the morning before I do. If you're there instead of me, they won't know what to think."

His words were reasonable, as was typical. But something about the way he spoke sent a trickle of awareness down the nape of Daisy's neck. It might have been the deepening of his tone or the slowing of his cadence or even the close proximity of his body to hers, but all at once, the air around them became charged. Not with shock or anger or unsaid questions. With…heat.

"I'm happy to take the sofa," she said quickly, before he could start the game she was sure he was set on embarking. "That isn't a problem."

"Yup, that's a possibility." With another wink, this one far more devilish than sardonic, he stepped closer. "Or… we could bunk together. Just to sleep, you understand."

Oh, she understood. She wondered, briefly, what his reaction would be if she called him on his…offer. Hmm. Maybe she should. If he wanted to play with fire, why not hand him the match? "You know, that's a great option. As long as you're certain it won't be too awkward."

"What's awkward about sleeping?" he asked in apparent innocence. "That is, if we're still talking about *only* sleeping?"

"We are." Narrowing the space between them by another inch, so they were only separated by the dog she held, and were close enough to—potentially, of course—kiss, she said, "The thing is, I've recently developed this small… idiosyncrasy, I'd guess you'd call it, and I'd hate for you to get the wrong impression."

Interest, amusement and, unless she missed her guess, desire flickered over him in varying degrees of intensity. "Keep talking," he said. "I can't wait to hear this."

"It's just that I find clothing so…restrictive." Fluttering her lashes, Daisy dropped her voice to a near whisper and looked him straight in those sexy-as-hell eyes of his. "I can't seem to sleep if I have anything at all covering me. So as long as you're okay with—"

Reid blinked once. Twice. "You sleep in the…?"

"Every single night." He seemed unable to talk, so being the kind and sensitive soul she was, she helped him out. "I think the sofa will be perfect. Don't you?"

"Right. The sofa."

"Though I could use a pillow and a few blankets."

"Right," Reid repeated. "I…ah…can get those for you."

"Thank you," she said in her best sweet-as-pie voice. "I would appreciate that."

He stayed put and continued to appraise her, his eyes slowly narrowing in contemplation. "Nice one, Daisy," he said after an abbreviated pause. "You almost had me."

Without uttering another syllable, Reid strode from the room. Daisy waited a full minute before collapsing on the sofa, before allowing the trembles to ripple along her skin and overtake her body. Her throat tightened and her stomach swam. How would she survive this?

She'd won this round due purely to surprise. That wouldn't happen again. If there were a next time, Reid would be fully prepared to call her on her bluff.

"I'm in trouble, Jinx," she whispered. Her dog's ears perked at the sound of her name and she butted her nose against Daisy's hand, begging for attention. Complying, Daisy stroked Jinx's head. "And not just your average type of trouble, either."

Nope. What she had was the cataclysmic, in-over-her-head, lucky-to-walk-away-in-one-piece type of trouble. And every speck of that trouble began and ended with Reid Foster.

The man she'd spent years trying to forget. The man who, despite her belief to the contrary, still claimed some part of her heart, her soul. She couldn't let him in again. Couldn't yield so much as an ounce of what she'd worked so hard to achieve, to become.

So, yeah. Trouble. In every which way that Daisy could see.

## Chapter Three

Far too early the next morning, Reid rolled over and stared at the clock, trying to decide if there were any point in attempting to get a little more shut-eye. He should. The day ahead promised to be challenging on myriad fronts, but he doubted he'd have any more luck in turning off his brain now than he had throughout the long, long night.

A certain flame-haired woman had occupied his thoughts, along with vivid—and unwanted—images of her asleep on the living room sofa in nothing but her birthday suit. He knew better, of course. Her parting shot, while an excellent and creative maneuver in putting an end to the juvenile game he'd stupidly started, was entirely false. This knowledge, however, hadn't stopped the images of a naked, prone Daisy from interfering with his ability to sleep.

He remembered her body with full and absolute clarity.

Reid groaned and punched his pillow. Why the hell had he stated they would live together? There were other options. Namely, he could have continued to be a presence in the girls' daily lives without the added difficulty of sleeping here. Easy enough to stop in after work, spend some time with Erin and Megan and return to his house when the girls were tucked into bed for the night. *That* would've been the sane option.

But no. The words *as of now, we're living together* had flown from his mouth, and once they had, he'd obstinately stuck to his guns. And even now, after a full night of considering the insanity of coexisting with Daisy, he wouldn't back out. The lines had been drawn.

He'd have to be careful, though. Within minutes of her arrival, he'd realized that whatever immunity he'd developed in regard to Daisy had weakened. She still held power over him. This concerned him. Unfortunately, it also fascinated him.

If she managed to squirrel in past his remaining defenses—if he made the almighty mistake of loving her again—he wasn't confident he'd recover when she left. The first go-round had nearly destroyed him. It had taken far too many months to locate the smallest, most fragile foothold in which to begin building the rest of his life on.

The idea of having to rebuild that foothold from scratch petrified him to the bone.

Frustrated with his seeming inability to push Daisy out of his mind for more than a few minutes, Reid chose to focus on the practicalities of what needed to occur. Due to the weather, he had—at minimum—an unexpected morning off.

Since the prior night's storm hadn't abated, and the high-velocity winds combined with the unrelenting snowfall had resulted in blizzard conditions, the mountain passes were closed. Later, once the weather calmed some, he and his fellow ski patrollers would sweep the mountain to determine the level of damage and where avalanche-control measures were required.

For now, though, he was relieved to have some additional personal time in which to help the girls grow more comfortable with their aunt. Also, he needed to apprise

Daisy of Erin and Megan's schedule and a few of their individual quirks.

Every now and again, Megan would decide she'd only wear clothes and eat foods of a certain color. Reid hadn't yet determined a reason for this behavior, but a few days ago she'd chosen blue. Most of her menu had revolved around blueberries.

Perhaps not the most balanced diet, but for one day, it had worked well enough.

And Erin, ever since her mother's death, often required something to hug whenever she was emotional or sitting for an extended length of time. A pillow or a stuffed animal or, once or twice, her backpack or her coat. Typically, this was handled without too much of a problem.

But if such an item wasn't close at hand at the wrong moment, she'd become fretful. To combat this, Reid unobtrusively ascertained that a stuffed animal was always nearby.

Major obstacles? No. But Daisy needed to be made aware of them, nonetheless.

Reid pushed out a long breath and tried to relax his muscles. If he fell asleep right this instant, he'd get an hour before the girls woke and the day began. Using a centering technique, he envisioned being on top of the mountain in perfect ski weather. The sun shone, the sky held the color of a robin's egg and the powder was…glorious.

In his head, he inhaled a lungful of cold, fresh air, felt the bite of the wind against his cheek and prepped his body for takeoff. He was a few short seconds from the push and the exhilarating ride down when the scene blinked out and Daisy appeared.

A naked and prone Daisy, on the sofa downstairs. The deep red hue of her hair in stark contrast with the pale warmth of her skin. Her blue-green eyes—filled with desire and love, need and longing—were directed at him. And a soft, seductive smile played upon her lips.

God. That look—that smile—had always done a number on him.

Forcing his eyes open, he gave up on the idea of sleep. His agenda now consisted of a cold shower and a pot of hot, strong coffee. Then he'd get started on breakfast and hope that today was one of Megan's "rainbow" days, which basically meant zero color preferences.

After that…well, he'd figure out the rest as needed.

Reid made the bed and grabbed a selection of clean clothes, including a pair of heavy work jeans and a thick forest-green cable-knit sweater, and headed for the upstairs bathroom. He'd no more than entered the hallway when a blur of color sped toward him with a…well, he didn't quite know what to call this particular canine noise.

Not a growl or a howl. Not really a bark, either. *Yip* was too small of a word, and didn't come close to the note of exuberant challenge erupting from the animal's throat.

"Really?" he said when Jinx collided with his ankles. Bare ankles, at that, since he wore a pair of boxer shorts. "This is the way it's going to be, huh? Every time you see me?"

The dog growled in reply and latched on to his left ankle in a surprisingly gentle grasp, as if searching for the pant leg she knew should be there. She didn't hurt him, didn't come close to actually biting, just grumbled and huffed with a few light gnaws tossed in for good measure.

More amused than annoyed, he let this go on for a good thirty seconds or so before deciding enough was enough. Walking carefully, to avoid squashing the crazy dog, he made his way down the hallway until he reached the bathroom.

"That's it," Reid said, as he turned on the light and put

his clothes on the counter. "The end of the road. Go find a ball or, I don't know, something to sniff."

Not to be deterred, Jinx trailed into the bathroom with him, darting around his legs as he moved and bounding toward his ankles whenever possible. If it weren't for the incessant growling, he'd think the beast just wanted to play.

"Listen up," he said, feeling somewhat idiotic for trying to reason with a dog. "I really hope it's only men you don't like, because two little girls live in this house. If you're this ornery around them, your visit will be awfully short."

Since Jinx seemed unimpressed by this morsel of logic, Reid guided the dog to the hallway using his ankles as bait. She was quicker than he was, though, and managed to squeeze back into the room the second he started closing the door.

Obviously, another tactic was called for.

Shaking his head, he picked up the dog. Jinx wiggled in his grasp and began growling in an elongated manner that damn near sounded as if she were trying to form the necessary words to talk to him. Ludicrous thought. He blamed his lack of sleep.

He hefted the dog up, so they were eye to eye. "Pay attention, pooch. We can do this the easy way and become friends or you can remain miserable for however long you're here. I guarantee you a happier visit if we're friends. A visit that might just include table scraps and belly rubs. Your choice. Friends or miserable living companions? Let me know."

And if a dog's eyes could narrow in deliberation, Reid would've sworn Jinx's did. Nonsensical, of course, but hell…that was what it looked like.

"That's right, you consider that." Petting the dog, he moved into the hallway and halfway down the stairs, where he put her down. "Find something to do. Or…I know, why don't you wake up Daisy and tell her to make breakfast. And coffee. Strong coffee."

He then retraced his steps without looking over his shoulder.

Thirty minutes later, showered and dressed but no more comfortable with his new living arrangements, he cautiously peered into the hallway. No sight or sound of Jinx.

Hell, if he could get a man-hating, irrational pooch to leave him alone, then he could certainly handle being around Daisy without repeating old patterns. Yesterday had been a shock to the system, that was all. Of course he'd reacted strongly.

Today was a different matter. She wouldn't be able to get to him on the same level that she had last night. Besides which, his memories were of a woman—no more than a girl, really—who likely no longer existed. He'd changed in the past eight years. Surely, she had, as well.

The tight, suffocating pressure encasing his chest lightened. Perhaps he should view this…madness as a blessing in disguise. He and Daisy could finally have the conversation they should have had years earlier. She could fully answer his questions and…well, ask her own once he confessed that he'd known the truth about her paternity before reading her letter.

He'd tell her all of it. The overheard argument. His decision to keep what he'd learned to himself until after their wedding. How his past self couldn't bear to see her hurt, couldn't allow her to go through even a second of what that knowledge would do to her in the days before they were to be married. How he'd wanted that moment of their lives to remain unmarred and whole.

Good enough reasons, Reid supposed, for keeping such a secret. But well-meaning didn't equate to what was right or just or honorable. And hell, he hadn't saved her from a damn thing.

She'd likely be spitting mad by his admittance. That was fine. Due and deserved, even. And he had his own brew to get off of his chest, over the way she'd ended their relationship and had just...walked into the sunset. *Without him.* Yeah. He had a lot to say on that front.

A difficult conversation for both of them, no doubt. But...restorative, too? Should be.

Confidence settled in, replacing every other sentiment he'd warred with throughout the night. His defenses were solid. His heart was safe.

His immunity, thank the Lord, remained intact.

Reid held this belief, this confidence, for the length of time it took to reach the kitchen from the upstairs hallway. She was there, dressed in an oversize purple flannel shirt worn as a nightgown, her elbows planted on the counter and her chin in her hands, while she stared at the slowly brewing coffeepot. And he was...mesmerized.

A simple scene. Nothing overtly sexy or out-of-the-ordinary about it. But his heart seemed to stop beating. His lungs seemed to stop taking in air. Every last muscle seemed to lose the ability to move. He was, for the next several seconds, frozen in time. Nothing but a statue, really—gifted with sight, thought and emotion.

In a rush of sensation, of raw awareness, his body started functioning again. His prior arguments fell away. They were meaningless and false. Nothing more than the desperate ramblings of a man who recognized he was a goner but wasn't prepared for surrender.

But now, Reid understood that a choice had never really existed. Without any further hesitation or the slightest whisper of doubt, he surrendered. And he knew that he would do whatever it took, whatever was in his power, to make certain that he saw this scene—Daisy, soft and rumpled from sleep—every morning for the rest of his life.

Well, hell.

Reid shook his head and swallowed a silent groan. Nope, he didn't have to worry about falling in love with Daisy again. That would be impossible.

He'd never stopped loving her to begin with.

There were men who could enter a room, not say a word, not do anything but stand in stillness, and every other person in that space would pause, turn and look. Reid Foster was such a man. He'd always had this quality, this…charismatic, magnetic aura, even as a boy.

So, despite her tiredness or the fact that she faced the opposite direction, Daisy sensed Reid's presence the instant he entered the kitchen. She didn't move or greet him or show any sign that she knew he stood behind her. Rather, she just waited.

For the coffee, which she desperately needed. For him, to set the tone, the cadence, of how they were going to start the day. In polite resignation or veiled hostility? With sexual innuendo or calm solidarity? She hoped for the solidarity. That somehow they would find a way to cross the minefield to band together, for the sake of Parker and her nieces, and become a…team.

But she wasn't holding her breath.

"Darlin', you must be a psychic. Or a genie," Reid said, his voice rich and warm and holding the tiniest thread of amusement. The warmth got to her the most, brought to mind all of those yesteryears she'd spent the entirety of the night trying to forget. "If any man on the face of God's green earth could use a cup of coffee right about now, that man would be me."

"Sorry. Not a psychic or a genie," Daisy replied, keeping her tone casual, confused by his. His warmth, his friendliness, his outward acceptance of her bore no resemblance to the man from last night. The question was…why? "Jinx tattled on you. Mentioned you were on the owly side, in need of sustenance and caffeine."

In truth, she'd been on her way to the kitchen when she overheard Reid's conversation with her dog. And she'd had to cover her mouth to stop from laughing out loud.

"That's...ah, rather perplexing," Reid said after a moment's hesitation.

"Which part?"

"All of it." Before she could blink, he was standing next to her, reaching into the cupboard for a couple of coffee mugs. "To start, I have no idea what *owly* means. To finish...your *dog* mentioned I wanted coffee and food? How does that work, exactly?"

"Owly means cranky." She shivered and wrapped her arms around herself, so Reid would think the reaction was due to being cold and not his close proximity. Too bad she couldn't fool herself. "And yes, Jinx and I have a method of communicating that defies logic."

"Uh-huh. Then why does she still hate men?" He looked around the room. "Where is she, anyway? Hiding out somewhere, ready to attack?"

"Nope. She's sleeping in the living room. Seems her quick sojourn outside this morning wore her out." Or maybe Jinx's feisty altercation with the man of the house had done that. Daisy could recall a few altercations—on the pleasant side of the equation—with Reid that had left her exhausted. "As to the other? I told you. I trained her to be that way."

"Right," he said matter-of-factly. "To protect you from the unwanted attention of men, I take it? Since you're a single woman living in L.A."

"Well, you know, can't be too careful." *Come on, coffee,* Daisy thought, staring at the ridiculously slow drip, drip, drip of the machine. She needed the distraction as much, if not more, as she needed the caffeine. "What about you?

Do you have a woman-hating dog waiting in the wings, to protect you from the unwanted attention of females?"

"Nah." Reid gave her a lazy, sexy sort of smile. She felt that smile all the way to her toes. Not good. Not good at all. "Haven't found the need."

"Gotcha." He hadn't found the need because he wanted female attention or…? Striking out that thought—fast— Daisy put a few inches of space between her and Reid. Just to simplify the mechanics of breathing. "Um. So, when do the girls usually wake up? Breakfast will be done soon. Baked French toast. Cinnamon. I hope they like cinnamon."

"Should be any minute. In fact—" Reid inhaled, as if drawing in strength "—we should probably have a quick discussion on how to handle their questions."

"Sure," she said, content to move into safer territory. "Shouldn't be too difficult. I'm their aunt, here to stay with them while their father recovers. But you'll still be here, so their schedules won't change too much in that regard." While this conversation didn't seem to be heading into the same danger zone as last night, she had every intention of standing her ground. "That is what we decided, right? Unless you've changed your mind about staying here?"

"Nope, can't say that I have." Reid grabbed the coffeepot and filled his mug and then hers. "But I thought we'd have some time while the girls were in school to talk things over. School's canceled for the day, though, so—"

"There's no school today?" a soft, tentative voice said from the other side of the kitchen. "And you're my aunt Daisy? Really and truly?"

"Hey there, peanut," Reid said. "And the answer is yes, to both of your questions."

Turning, Daisy took a good, long look at her younger niece, Megan. And her heart melted into a big, wet puddle. Megan's doe-brown eyes and fine light blond hair reminded Daisy of the girls' mother. Sweet and fragile and innocent beyond words.

"Morning, Megan," she said brightly. "And yes, I'm your aunt Daisy."

"I don't remember you." Then, shyly dropping her gaze, Megan said, "But I sleep with the doll you gave me for Christmas almost every night. I named her Holly."

"Holly is a wonderful name, and I'm happy you like her so much." Crossing the room, Daisy kneeled in front of the little girl and resisted the almost overwhelming desire to pull her close for a hug. "It's okay that you don't remember me. You were only two the last time I saw you. But I'm glad we can be together now, and I promise we'll have lots of fun."

Long lashes blinked. Ever so slowly, Megan raised her chin until her eyes met Daisy's. A small, hesitant smile appeared. "I like fun. Erin does, too." And then, as if worried that Daisy might not know—or remember—who Erin was, she said, "Erin is my sister. She's seven. I'm five. And she has hair that looks like yours."

"Does she?" Daisy knew this, of course, as Parker sent a photo of the girls with his Christmas card each year. "The red hair comes from your grandmother. My—and your daddy's—mom. Just like your beautiful blond hair comes from—"

Uh-oh. Was it taboo to mention Bridget? She glanced toward Reid, hoping he'd give her some type of a signal, but his attention was focused on Megan.

"My mommy," Megan elaborated, her voice carrying a note of pride. Sadness, too, but that was natural. "I…I don't remember her much. But Daddy says that all the time about my hair."

Daisy's throat closed in emotion. "Yes, that's what I was going to say. That you remind me of your mother," she said gently. "Ready for breakfast?"

Before Megan could reply, Reid—who had quietly watched their exchange while sipping his coffee—asked, "Is this a color day, peanut?"

A curious question. Just one more to ask later. And, not that she'd admit this, but her few seconds of talking with Megan had made it all-too-obvious how badly Daisy required Reid's input. She was even…grateful for any help he was willing to give. Now, more than ever, it seemed essential that she didn't screw this up.

Megan wrinkled her nose in thought before giving her head a decisive shake no.

"Well, then. A rainbow day it is," Reid said easily. "Why don't you run upstairs and get your sister while your aunt and I serve breakfast?"

"Okay." Megan started to reach for Daisy and then stopped, as if unsure. Daisy opened her arms and waited, sensing the decision needed to remain in Megan's hands. One second passed. Two seconds. Three… And then, all at once, the little girl pushed herself forward and hugged her tight. "I'm glad you're here," she whispered before letting go.

"I'm glad I'm here, too." After Megan dashed out of the kitchen in search of her sister, Daisy said, "That went better than I expected. She's a sweet little thing, isn't she?"

"Yup, she is." Reid began setting the table. Taking his lead, Daisy removed the baking dish of French toast from the oven. A few minutes of not-too-awkward silence ensued. Once he'd poured the orange juice, he said, "You were good with her, Daisy. And…well, I've reached a decision I feel is only fair to share with you."

"Um. Thank you." An unexplainable shiver of apprehension and foreboding brought a coating of goose bumps to Daisy's arms. "What decision might that be?"

"Well, it's like this," Reid said in a slow and purposeful cadence. "I walked in here this morning all set to make the best of this situation, and there you were, hunkered over the coffeepot in that flannel getup you're wearing. And I was smacked with a…profound realization."

Heat, instant and intense, appeared dead-center in her stomach. "Profound?"

"Significantly so." Facing her, Reid gently tipped her chin so that she had no choice but to look into his eyes. "To me, anyway."

*Trouble.* "Are we speaking of the coffee?" she asked, going for brevity. "Because while I agree that the first cup in the morning is important, to call it profound is—"

"No, honey. Not the coffee." While he spoke, he traced her lips with his fingers as if he'd done so every day for years on end, eliciting another series of shivers. From the touch itself, yes, but also from the waves of desire traveling through. "This is about us, Daisy. You and I."

She tried to think. Lord, did she try. "Our past? We can have that conversation. I mean, now probably isn't the best time, with the girls and breakfast and—"

"We will. But no, this isn't the right time." His voice held assurance. Confidence. "I'm speaking of now, not our past. And, sweetheart, you should know that in my opinion we—meaning you and I—are not done."

"Is this another game?" Swallowing, hard, she pulled herself free. "If so, I'm not interested in games, Reid. I told you last night that I'm here for Parker and my nieces, not to…not for any other reason."

"I'm not playing a game."

"Then what is this about?" Her heart hammered against her breastbone and her mouth went dry. "Because if you're alluding to—"

"Now see, that is exactly what I'm not doing." An easy, carefree grin lit his countenance. All innocence and charm. "My goal here is to be very clear about my intentions."

"And those intentions are…what?"

"The same as they were seven years and nine months ago." Determination firmed his jaw, straightened the line of his mouth. "If you recall, you mentioned in your good-bye letter—you know the one, from our wedding day?— that you still wanted to marry me, just not on *that* day."

Where could he possibly be going with this? "I thought we established that this wasn't the proper time to have this conversation. But yes, I...wrote something along those lines."

"Good, glad you remember." He leaned against the counter in a too-casual-to-be-truly-casual pose. "You also stated that you hoped—if fate was on our side—we might have a second chance at forever," he said, his tone quiet. Focused. "Do you recall those sentiments, as well?"

"Um...I...yes, but—" Syllable by syllable, his words crashed into her brain with the force of an out-of-control semitruck. "Why are you asking these questions?"

"Because what that letter boils down to is a contract. At the very least, a promise from you to me." Satisfaction and pleasure whooshed into his expression, his eyes, his very being. "You owe me a wedding, Daisy. And I plan to collect."

"Wh-what?" Huh-uh. Impossible. She'd heard him wrong. "I owe you what?"

"A wedding, Daisy. *Our* wedding."

"Is this a joke?" she asked, finding her voice. "Has to be a joke, right? Because no man anywhere would decide to marry a woman he hasn't seen for *eight* years."

Not to mention, marrying the woman who'd left him standing at the altar.

"Oh, I'm not joking." Reid pushed himself off the counter and strode to the large calendar hanging on the opposite wall. "How does April sound to you?" he asked, flipping the pages as he spoke. "Though, Cole and Rachel's wedding is the nineteenth. Is March too soon? Probably. I'd like Parker to be there. I suppose we could shoot for May again, but—"

"Payback? Is this a form of retribution?" When he didn't respond, when he did nothing but stare at her in a mix of pleasure and confidence, her knees wobbled enough that she had to move to one of the kitchen chairs to sit down. "What's the punch line, Reid?"

"Love," he said simply.

"Do you realize how insane you sound?"

"Marriage."

"Delusional, too. And there isn't any way I'm buying in to—"

"Maybe even a few children down the road." He let go of the calendar and took the chair next to Daisy. "I've always thought three kids was a nice, round number. What do you think?"

Love. Marriage. Children. Everything she'd once wanted with this man. Everything she'd once ran away from. Everything she'd long since decided wasn't for her.

"You can't really expect me to believe that you're serious. And…and this isn't funny," she said, speaking slowly and clearly. In order to get through that megathick skull of his. "You're joking. Or playing a game. Or you're out for revenge. Or—"

"None of the above," Reid said firmly. "I'm not only serious about this, Daisy, I'm committed. Guess I'll be working on proving that to you."

She had more to say. Much, much more, but the sounds of two little girls running down the stairs made any further discussion impossible. He was joking. He *had* to be joking.

But what if…what if he wasn't?

## Chapter Four

The loss of Reid's sanity didn't feel as frightening as he would have expected. Odd, perhaps, but his sudden decision to pursue Daisy seemed almost inescapable. Preordained by fate, even. *That* was the instinct he'd fought against all night.

Of course, he hadn't planned on stating his intentions quite so explicitly. Rather, he thought he'd announce his interest and his desire to get to know her again, and then go about the business of courting her. But in the blink of an eye, the details of her letter had appeared in his mind. *She* had declared it doubtful that her love for him would disappear.

*She* had written her hope that they'd have another chance. Those were her words, not his.

So, no, the idea of planning a wedding hadn't occurred to him until that second. But damn, he sort of liked the idea. Insane? Oh, hell yeah. High-risk? Yup, that, too. She could very well shoot him down from now until the actual wedding date and return to her life in California without so much as a glance over her shoulder. Or, he supposed, with or without a letter of goodbye. And hell, that would be rough, going through that mess all over again.

Truth was, though, he'd rather give this crazy idea everything he had and hope for a superior outcome than not try at all. Hope offered possibilities.

He wanted those possibilities. Because, whether he'd realized it until now or not, his gut told him they belonged together. And what better way to proceed than with purpose and intent?

Daisy wouldn't stick around forever. And, unless this aspect of her personality had changed, she didn't pay much attention to the subtle. A wedding, though? Nothing subtle about a wedding. That would grab and hold her notice—it already had—and while they were dancing around that topic, he'd begin tackling the obstacles, one by one, they'd need to confront.

And, if he had his say, move beyond.

Swallowing another gulp of coffee, Reid leaned back in his chair at the kitchen table and winked at Daisy, who was in the middle of a conversation with the girls.

She faltered, narrowed her eyes slightly, regained her focus and said, "Since there isn't any school today, I thought we could play a few games. How does that sound?"

Megan nodded enthusiastically but didn't try to talk through her chewing. Erin, on the other hand, shook her head and frowned. "I don't want to play a game."

"That's okay," Daisy said without pause. "We can do something else. Maybe…draw pictures for your dad? Or some get-well cards?"

"He likes our pictures and cards," Megan said. "He says we're artists."

"No. We colored pictures and cards for Daddy yesterday." Erin stabbed her fork into a bite-size square of her French toast. Glancing at Reid, she said, "Didn't we?"

"We did, but I'm sure your father would love more," Reid said, surprised by Erin's quick opposition to Daisy's suggestions. "Is there something else you'd like to do today, monkey?"

"Build a snowman," she said instantly. "With *you.*"

Meaning, he guessed, not with Daisy. Hmm. "Well," he said, trying to figure out the reason for the child's negativity. Erin didn't easily warm up to new folks, so he'd expected some shyness on her part. But he hadn't seen this coming. "It's a little too wild out there for building snowmen right now. Probably best if we focus on indoor ideas."

"You can read us a book," Erin said, without looking at Daisy. "Or...or—"

"But I want to play with Aunt Daisy!" Megan said. "And books are for bedtime."

"Not always," Daisy said, her voice warm and relaxed. "Books are good for anytime you want to read—or hear—a story. So, Reid can read to Erin, and you and I—" Daisy pointed to Megan "—can do something else. Games or coloring or whatever you want."

"No!" Erin's mouth formed into a pout. "We always play together."

"That isn't true," Megan said. "So don't say it is!"

"Almost always, so it is true!" Erin vaulted from her chair. "I'm older and Daddy isn't here and I'm in charge. R-Reid is going to tell us a story and *she* can do something else!"

"Whoa, now," Reid interjected, taken aback by Erin's vehemence. Even so, he kept his tone calm, modulated. "First off, kiddo, you don't get to dictate what Megan does, and I think you know that." He waited for Erin to nod. When she did, he added, "Okay, good. Also, there isn't any call to be rude. Please apologize."

"Sorry, Megan," Erin said quietly.

"Okay," Megan said. "Just don't say stuff that isn't true."

"But we almost always—"

"Girls, let's not start a new argument when we're in the

middle of making up." Reid paused and looked at Erin. "Is there something you'd like to say to your aunt now?"

"Not really," Erin said, sounding far more like a teenager than a seven-year-old girl. "I just don't want to play with her today."

"You know that isn't what I meant," Reid said. "Please apologize to your aunt."

"Reid," Daisy said quickly. "She doesn't have to—"

"Yes, she does. Parker might not be here at the moment, but his rules still hold," Reid said, attempting to achieve the right balance of maintaining boundaries and showing compassion. "You tell me, Erin. What would your dad say if he was here right now?"

Erin's chin quivered. "That it is okay to show how we feel but it isn't okay to be rude or…or hurtful to other people."

"Yup, that's right," Reid said. "And what do you think he would want you to do?"

Blinking rapidly, as if to stop herself from crying, Erin looked from Reid to Daisy and then at the floor. "I'm s-sorry for being rude."

"It's really okay, Erin. This is new and sudden," Daisy said softly, looking as if she might burst into tears herself. "Thank you for the apology. And…I hope we can spend some time together later. If you want to, that is."

Shrugging, Erin spun on her heel and just about flew from the kitchen. Megan dropped her fork on her plate and started to stand, her intent to follow her sister fairly obvious. She hesitated and glanced at Reid with questions in her eyes.

He nodded and she took off. Sighing, Reid raked his fingers over his short hair. He wanted to sit down with Erin right now and reassure her that everything was going to be fine. But she needed to calm down some before she'd be willing to share whatever was bothering her.

So he'd wait. Not too long, though.

"She isn't normally like that, Daisy," he said. "I'll go talk with her in a few minutes, see if I can work out what the issue is." Daisy nodded and busied herself with clearing the dishes from the table. "She'll adjust, I'm sure. Just give her a little time."

"I hope so, and I will," Daisy said. "I...I almost see myself when I look at Erin."

"Not surprised. You resemble one another."

"The hair, yes. But she has her mother's eyes, like her sister, and the narrow Lennox nose." Now at the sink, Daisy began rinsing off the breakfast dishes. "If it wasn't for our red hair, I'm not sure anyone would see a physical resemblance. There was just something about the way she looked at me that seemed familiar."

"It's more than the color of your hair." Surprised that Daisy hadn't yet lit into him over his wedding proclamation, Reid gathered the drinking glasses and considered how to proceed. Go full bore or take a slower, gentler approach? "You share similar mannerisms and a propensity toward separating yourself from most other folks."

Daisy gave him a sidelong glance that suggested she was rearing up to clock him on the jaw. "Are you insinuating that my niece and I are self-absorbed?"

"Maybe. But only in the best possible light."

"Not quite sure how you can get 'best possible light' out of self-absorbed."

"Perhaps 'choosy' is a better description," he said, joining her at the sink. She continued to rinse and, as she did, he loaded the dishwasher. "Nothing wrong with that."

And there wasn't. Daisy tended to keep others at a distance until she determined if they could be trusted with her thoughts, dreams...that inner world of hers. Erin was the same. Most folks were to a certain extent, but some were more cautious, more particular, in who they let in.

"Honestly, I think she took one look at me and decided she doesn't like me." Pain and sorrow deepened the blue in Daisy's eyes. "I should've tried harder before."

"She hasn't decided anything as of yet." Reid didn't comment on the rest. There wasn't any reason to rub additional salt into the wound. He'd done a good enough job of that last night. "And you're here now. It isn't too late to build a connection."

"Maybe, but it seems I have my work cut out for me." Sidestepping him, she wiped off the table and resituated the chairs. When she finished, she faced him and arched an eyebrow. "And just to avoid any confusion, I want to be absolutely clear that I'm not going to allow you to indulge in some stupid game. I do not owe you a wedding. End of discussion."

Well, then. Full bore it was. "I believe I was already clear when I said that you did. And this discussion is far from over."

"Stop." Narrowed eyes met his. With a stubborn lift of her chin, she took one long step toward him. "This wedding talk of yours is nonsense. As I just said, I have my work cut out for me. I do not have time to deal with…with whatever you're trying to prove."

"We both have a lot of work in front of us," he said. "Planning our last wedding took close to a year, so supposing we settle on May, we still only have a couple of months." Unable to stop himself, he grinned. "March or April will leave us with even less time."

"There is nothing to plan!" Now the green in her eyes took precedence over the blue. From anger, no doubt, but desire had always had the same effect. "You are not due a wedding."

"We'll have to agree to disagree. A contract was made, a promise was implied." Shrugging, he said, "And, Daisy, you reneged on both."

"Is this because you want to *talk* about what I did? If so, just say that! We can talk. Right now, for however long you'd like. Otherwise, you need to...cease and desist."

"Sorry." He whisked his thumb along the soft curve of her cheek, her skin warming beneath his touch. "That's the one thing I cannot do."

"Assuming we went by your incredibly flawed logic," she said, flicking his hand off her face, "I still wouldn't owe you a damn thing. I returned the ring, which then signified the end of the so-called contract and my implied promise. Even if I hadn't, even if your argument held any weight whatsoever, the statute of limitations would have long since expired."

"Ah, well, I don't believe there is any such thing as a statute of limitation for affairs of the heart. Love, in my book, is one of those forever types of deals." Pushing his fingers into her hair, he gently tipped her head back. "Want to know what I'm thinking about right this instant?"

Her tongue darted out to lick her lips. A little move that just about killed him right then and there. "Oh, I don't know," she said. "That you should call a therapist?"

"For premarital counseling?"

"To have your head examined!"

"I'm compelled to kiss you," he said, allowing her the opportunity to shove him away. Slap him. Kick him. Or... agree to be kissed. "If you stay this close, I won't be able to resist."

"Why do you want to kiss me?" Neither her voice nor her gaze wavered, but the green in her eyes darkened another delicious degree. Anger or desire? "And why now?"

"I can't remember a time I haven't wanted to kiss you," he said, speaking the truth that was, depending on the day, a blessing or a curse. "As to why? Because you make me love you, Daisy. You always have, and I suspect you always will. I'm done trying to escape the inescapable."

"Sweet talk will get you nowhere. Other than proving you've lost your mind."

"I'm not arguing that possibility at all."

"Finally, we agree on something!" she said, yanking herself backward. "What is this really about? You couldn't wait to get me out of here last night, and now...now—"

"Kiss me, Daisy."

A pale pink flush stole over her cheeks. "You want a kiss?"

"That I do."

She stared at him. He stared right back, intrigued by where this exchange might lead, by the woman herself. This Daisy wasn't the exact same Daisy he remembered, and that was good—he wasn't the same, either. Not being able to predict what she might say or do held enormous appeal. More so than he would've thought.

"I'll kiss you," she said. "But only if you promise not to move. Not even an inch."

Okay, that seemed interesting. "Sure," he said. "I promise not to move."

Standing on her tiptoes, she brushed her lips along his jaw. Her touch was slow and seductive, potent and powerful. So much so, he had to use every ounce of his resolve to stand still, to let Daisy take control of...whatever happened next.

The warmth of her breath licked against his skin and a groan of pleasure, anticipation, caught in his throat. Her breasts were tight against his chest, her hands rested on his upper arms, and the softness—the light, flowery scent—of her hair tickled and teased his senses. His entire body resonated with awareness as her mouth skimmed the lines of his face, moving from his jaw to his cheek to his ear, before returning to his jaw to restart the journey.

Every second, every glide of her lips, every area their bodies met, was absolute torture. Absolute perfection. *Yes.*

This woman belonged with him, he with her, and nothing could alter that basic fact. Reid would, if necessary, drag the moon from the sky and wrap it in a solid gold, diamond-studded bow to convince her of this belief.

Daisy exhaled a breath and pushed away, putting far too much room in between them. Wiping her mouth with the palm of her hand, she said, "There. You got your kiss. Several of them, in fact. Can we end this ludicrous game now?"

"Again...this is not a game. Look," he said, carefully choosing his words, "I hadn't planned on this. When I found you in the living room with that crazy dog of yours, I wanted to feel nothing. I wanted to be able to send you on your way and get on with my life."

"And that reaction is totally logical. I understand why you might prefer my absence over my presence. I...I get that." She squeezed her eyes shut, pursed her lips and blew out a breath. "But if you're not playing some twisted game meant to shove me out the door, then I can't make any sense of your change in behavior or your sudden insistence to...to..."

"Marry you?"

"Y-yes."

"It's simple." Metaphorically, he reached for the moon and yanked it into his grasp. God help him, he really was going to risk it all. "I thought I had gotten you out of my system, that I was long over you. But the truth is, I love you, Daisy. Then and now. Still and forever."

Gasping, she shook her head in a physical rejection of his claim. Okay, not what a man wanted to see when he declared his love for a woman, but he figured she had the right to her shock and denial. He hadn't gotten over his own shock as of yet.

"I... You don't love me, Reid."

"But I do."

"You can't." Her already pale skin whitened a shade.

Maybe two shades. "You don't know who I am. You didn't know me before, either. You couldn't when…when I didn't even know myself. I'm not sure you loved me then, so to say that you love me now isn't…plausible."

"That's close to what I thought earlier, and if I were standing in your shoes, I'd feel the same." He wasn't an idiot. He knew he sounded as if he were off his rocker. How to explain what he didn't fully understand himself? He just…*knew*. "I might not know how you spend your Friday nights or if you still curse when you drive, but, Daisy…I know *you*."

"You…you're caught up in the past or something. That's all this is." Dipping her chin, she focused on the tile floor. "I remember the way we were, and seeing you again has been intense. For both of us. So I think you're…stuck in what you—we—once wanted."

She could be right, he supposed, but he wasn't convinced. His intuition had swung into high gear, and he'd learned to listen when that happened. Doing so had saved his hide—and had helped him save other people's hides—on more than one occasion. Often in the middle of treacherous, life-or-death scenarios on the mountain.

Not everyone formed decisions the way that Reid and his family did. The Fosters trusted their guts, paid attention to their hearts, and would just as soon take the proverbial leap off a cliff based solely on these convictions. They did not sit idly by and do nothing.

Reid had sat idly by, though.

Seven years and nine months ago, he'd ignored his gut and had let Daisy go without a fight. Out of guilt and anger for his own poor, albeit well-meaning, actions. Out of pride. Out of his frustration and devastation over her departure and lack of trust in him…in them. Nope, he hadn't listened to his instincts then, but he damn well would now.

"I'm sorry you don't yet believe me, but I'm certain of

what I want. I won't be giving up, and I won't be walking away. Which means," he said, purposely drawing out the words, the moment, "I'm going to move forward and plan our wedding."

"Insane," she muttered. "Completely, unbelievably nuts."

"Possibly," he said. "But that doesn't alter my intent."

"Are you going to haul me to the church, whether I agree or not?" The bite was back in her voice, her demeanor, and energy snapped in the air between them. "Or do I have an actual say in this demented plan of yours?"

"Whether you show up or not is completely up to you, as it should be," he said, choosing to let the demented comment slide. "And naturally, you have a say in our wedding plans. I'm flexible on the details, darlin', so whatever you want will likely be fine with me."

"Flexible on the details? Whatever I want, huh?"

"We can run off to Vegas, if you'd like."

Irritation, irrefutable and complete, cascaded over her features. With a glare so heated it could melt every inch of snow currently covering the ground, she said, "Go for it, Reid. Spend your time, waste your money and plan a freaking wedding. But understand this—you can perfect every last detail, but you'll still be missing a bride!"

That, Reid knew, was the risk. Masking his concern, he went with a laid-back, no-big-deal sort of shrug. "Got it. Completely understood. I just happen to think you'll change your mind."

"Wow. Are you really that sure of yourself?"

"Sure enough." Reid removed the calendar from the wall and, like he had earlier, flipped through the pages. "Now, the only question I have is…what date—if you *were* to show up—works well for you? Or should I go ahead and choose the wedding date on my own?"

"You can't be—" She yanked the calendar from his grasp. A quick flip brought her to the month of May. "If you insist on continuing with this lunacy, let's dive head-first into the crazy pool, shall we? I choose May sixth."

*May sixth.* Their original wedding date. "Romantic notion."

"Isn't it, though?" She threw the calendar in the air toward him. He caught it, searched for and found the applicable month. With a slight toss of her head, she said, "There's a full-circle appeal, don't you think? Two weddings, same date, no bride at either one."

"Or you could marry me and we could be happy for the rest of our lives," he said, staring at the calendar. "Possible dilemma, though. May sixth falls on a Tuesday this year. Do you think that will present an issue for our guests?"

Tap, tap, tap went her foot. "I think 'our' guests will have a lot more to gossip about than having to attend a farce of a wedding on a Tuesday."

"Hmm." He pretended to mull over the idea. "Actually, this is supposed to be our special day, correct? If your heart is set on the sixth, we'll make it work."

"Reid," she said in utter calmness.

"Yes, honey?"

"Don't do this. Why complicate an already complicated situation?"

"Don't do…oh. You've already changed your mind about the date?" He scratched his jaw, feigning innocence. "That was fast. Still feeling May, or are you thinking a different month altogether? I hear June is one of the most popular months for weddings."

"You're…incorrigible and…and—" Snapping her mouth shut, she gave him a final withering glare and stalked from the kitchen. A few minutes later, he heard the slam of the downstairs bathroom door and, a few minutes after that, the rush of water through the pipes.

Whistling, Reid rehung the calendar on the wall. Most folks might consider what had just occurred as a dozen check marks on the con side of a pro-and-con list. But despite Daisy's aggravation, he felt lighter, more hopeful and content than he had in years.

Yup, she'd blustered and put up a fuss—who wouldn't?— and had, perhaps rightly so in this matter, decreed him a lunatic. What she hadn't done was outright say she no longer loved him. And that…well, he was about as sure as he could be that Daisy would not have hidden or veiled such a sentiment if she already knew her feelings.

Hope existed. For now, that was more than enough to keep Reid centered. After all, where hope lived, any damn thing on the face of the earth could happen. Even a wedding ceremony that the bride-to-be hadn't yet agreed to attend.

She had, though, set the date.

So May sixth it was. Perhaps this time, Reid wouldn't stand alone at the altar…waiting for a woman who never appeared.

Oh…just oh! How could she have forgotten about this side of Reid's temperament? She'd rarely argued with him in the past, but the very few times she had always resulted in Reid getting exactly what he wanted. Because she'd give in. Every single time.

But not on this.

Daisy dug out her hair dryer and plugged it into the wall socket in the bathroom. Really, who did he think he was, commandeering a wedding without her approval—without so much as a proposal!—and stating his love for her hadn't died? Then and now, he'd said. Still and forever.

Well. Okay. She couldn't deny the sweetness of that part of this entire fiasco. Couldn't deny the warm glow those words had given her. But, sweet or not, that didn't mean she'd bought in to any of his…ramblings. She hadn't. She wouldn't. She… Damn it, why was he doing this?

Powering on the hair dryer, Daisy bent her head and tried

to let go of the twist of anxiety tightening her stomach. If he weren't engaged in some form of payback, if this truly did not fall into the "game" category—and she no longer thought he was or that it did—then what was he up to? She just didn't know, and frankly, didn't want to waste any additional energy figuring it out.

There were other areas that required her attention. The areas that had brought her here in the first place. And she couldn't allow Reid—or anything to do with Reid—to cloud that purpose.

Okay, then. She couldn't control his actions, but she could control her *reactions*. No matter what he decided to do in regard to this ridiculous wedding of his, she'd maintain her distance, remain calm and wait for him to come to his senses.

He would. He *had* to. Because if he didn't, if he continued on in the manner he had this morning, she might begin to believe. In him. In his words. In…all of it.

And that could not, under any circumstances, happen.

As luck would have it, Daisy had her own mixture of confusion and memories creating havoc with her head, resurrecting all of those feelings she once had—and those that still existed—in her heart. Unlike Reid, though, after a full sleepless night of intense contemplation, she'd convinced herself that the rush of emotion, the strength of her attraction toward him, rested in the history they shared. None of it had to do with today.

Or so she hoped, because she did not do well with romantic entanglements.

She'd had a few relationships over the years, and each of them had ended in the same disastrous way. No, she'd never fallen for another man with the depth she'd once loved Reid, but she had cared for other men. Romantically. And with that care came her strong, strong desire to make them happy. To put their needs above her own.

Not such a bad thing, she supposed. Successful, loving relationships demanded give-and-take. For Daisy, though, she…lost herself in the giving, in the trying to be whatever she thought the other person wanted or needed her to be. Until she all but forgot who *she* was.

Easy to understand that this mentality came from her childhood, from all of her attempts to gain her father's love and appreciation. Comprehension, however, did not solve the issue.

So, several years ago now, she'd stopped dating. Entirely.

Without thought, she touched her fingers to her lips, recalling the flurry of small, light kisses she'd bestowed on Reid, the incredibly strong desire for their bodies to meld together in the way that they used to…for the completeness of being with Reid. A wholeness that held great appeal but had likely been false, based on *her* inabilities, *her* insecurities.

No. She wouldn't fall down that rabbit hole. Couldn't. *Memories* had induced her desire. *Memories* were to blame. Historical data that her body had pushed to the surface due to the intense force of being home, of seeing and dealing with Reid.

In a week or two, the turbulence would settle, their emotions would recalibrate into something less extreme and all of this crazy talk would end. Neither one of them would be worse for the wear, and she'd return to her life in California without any regrets. Old or new.

All she had to do until then was draw an impassable line in the sand and keep to her side. Well, that and let him do whatever he was going to do on his side…without reacting. As long as she didn't start to believe in his madness, she'd get through just fine.

A gurgle of choked laughter escaped from her throat. What in the hell was he up to?

## Chapter Five

Pausing outside of the girls' bedroom, Daisy pressed her palm against her stomach—which very much felt as if she'd swallowed a handful of jumping beans—and silently counted to ten. The door was closed, but she heard the murmur of chatter easily enough.

Naturally, the deep timbre of Reid's voice proved the most distinctive, the most penetrating. A voice, Daisy believed, she'd recognize in the middle of a noisy crowd regardless of where she was, or if she expected him to be there.

She would just…know.

There were moments spread throughout her years in California where she'd hear a man speak, and something—his tone or the cadence or the manner in which a certain word was said—would have her think, just for a second, that Reid was nearby. Even as she'd searched the restaurant or the beach or wherever she happened to be, she would know that the voice she'd heard, despite its similarity in some context, did not belong to Reid Foster.

But she always looked. *Always.*

And, when she found the man whose voice had caused her breath to catch and her pulse to race—a man who was, of course, a stranger—she'd close her eyes and wait for the taste of bitter disappointment to fade. Maybe a few seconds. Maybe a few minutes. She would then continue on until the next time a man's voice captured her awareness.

Fortunately, this only occurred once or twice or, at the most, three times each year.

Annoyed with herself for thoughts she did not need to have, Daisy kneeled down to hoist Jinx into her arms. She'd cajoled the dog into following her for a couple of reasons. Mainly, she wanted the initial interaction between her nieces and Jinx to go well. In addition, she hoped her dog—who, unlike her feelings toward men, adored children—would accomplish what Daisy had not and create an instantaneous connection with Erin.

Kids loved animals, didn't they? Most of them, anyway?

"I need your help here," Daisy whispered to Jinx. "I need you to please, please ignore the man in the room and allow two little girls to love you. Can you do that, sweets?"

Jinx, sadly, didn't reply.

Twisting the doorknob, she walked into Erin and Megan's bedroom, and instantly loved what she saw. Pale-hued, multicolored butterflies covered the bottom half of the light mint-green painted walls. Billowy pink curtains framed the two long, narrow windows—one of which served as a centerpiece between the girls' beds—and a corner shelf displayed books, dolls and a small television set. Groups of stuffed animals, a child-size table and chairs, along with other various toys and activities were strategically scattered around the room. The framed pictures of rainbows and flowers and ladybugs added to the carefree joy the space evoked.

It was a perfect place for two little girls to call their own.

At the moment, Erin and Megan were stretched out on their stomachs on one of the twin beds, while Reid sat on the other with an open book on his lap. Ah. Reading time.

"Join us?" Reid asked with a smile. "I'll even let you read if you promise to use different voices for each of the characters. The girls insist, you see."

So confident. So freaking at ease. How could he sit there with that smile, that relaxed, almost satisfied attitude, after the exchange they'd shared?

For the sake of the girls, of course. And if he could pull off a laid-back, happy-with-the-current-world demeanor, then…she could, as well. Or she could try, anyway.

"Maybe later," Daisy said, striving for the same level of upbeat cheerfulness. Lowering herself onto the pink-carpeted floor, she smiled at Erin and Megan. They'd noticed Jinx right off, she knew, as their eyes were glued to the dog. "Her name is Jinx. Want to meet her?"

Nodding exuberantly, Megan slid from the bed and sort of half skidded, half tumbled into position next to Daisy. Jinx instantly freed herself from Daisy's hold and fell on Megan with all the love only a dog can give, without so much as a growl in Reid's direction.

It seemed the adoration of a little girl outweighed the annoying presence of a man. *Good.* Daisy had worried that Jinx might scare the girls if Jinx had gone after Reid like she had last night.

"Now I feel like chopped liver," Reid muttered, with more than a smidge of humor. "She really just hates men, huh?"

"Yep. And if you were chopped liver, she'd consider that a significant improvement," Daisy said, enjoying the look of pure delight on Megan's face. Then, glancing at Erin, who hadn't budged so much as an inch, Daisy gestured toward Jinx. "Feel like getting in on this?"

"No, thank you." Erin scooted across the bed for a pillow, which she squeezed tight to her chest. A yearning, so vivid that Daisy could identify the look from where she sat, swam in the girl's gaze. "Megan can play with…Jinx. I…I'm fine."

At a loss as to what to say or do, Daisy said, "Okay. There isn't any rush."

By now, Jinx and Megan were acting as if they were long-lost best friends. Megan's arms were wrapped around the dog, and Jinx continually nudged her nose into Megan's long, silky hair, bestowing the child's cheek with a sloppy kiss whenever the opportunity presented itself.

"Looks like your sister's having a lot of fun, monkey," Reid said casually. "I think you'd have a lot of fun, too. And…last I heard, you've been wanting a dog for a long while."

Erin shook her head and hugged her pillow harder, her despondency and stubbornness at not allowing herself something she so obviously wanted at war with one another.

"All righty, then," Reid said in concern. "The choice is yours."

The weight of it all—Megan's happy giggles as opposed to Erin's determined withdrawal, Reid's claims of love, her brother's accident and even her return to Steamboat Springs—combined to increase the invisible pressure on Daisy's shoulders.

She wasn't prepared. In any way.

True enough. But she had determined that her stance on Reid, and the reality of being back in her hometown, would both probably become easier within a few days. And okay, once she visited with her brother, her worries regarding his health would hopefully decrease. She might even glean some information that would help her better understand Erin.

Until then, the best she could do for Erin was to remain calm, positive, and to pay attention to her signals. In this second, what Erin needed the most was Daisy out of her bedroom.

"Okay, you goofs," Daisy said, rising to her feet. "I interrupted reading time, so I'll take Jinx downstairs and let you three get back to it."

"Stay!" Megan said, still giggling. "You and Jinx can listen to the story."

"That," Reid said, "is a great idea. No reason to run off."

Hmm. Was that an innocent, no-harm-meant gibe, or a planned one meant to remind Daisy of her transgression? With most folks, she would lean toward innocent. But with Reid, their past and his current state of madness—who knew?

"Oh, I'm not running off." She gave Reid a pointed look. "I still have to retrieve my suitcase from the car, and I have a few phone calls to make. Work and such."

Sort of true. The suitcase portion, if not the other.

Daisy worked as a freelance personal assistant, and usually only accepted short-term positions that appealed to her on one level or another. Some people required intense, hands-on motivation. Others required someone to function as a mediator between their personal and professional lives. She might help one client plan a social function, or assist another with organization, or manage an executive's schedule with the precision of a brain surgeon.

She'd even, a time or two, posed as a girlfriend.

What most of her assignments had in common was the similarity in clients, if not in job duties. Sure, she needed to earn a living, but whenever she could, she tended to work with people who were at a crossroads—either personally or professionally—and had experienced some type of an obstacle. People who were trying to get their life back on track.

Fortunately, in Los Angeles, the high demand for such a range of services never lessened. And the pay was good. When Parker had phoned, she'd literally just ended one such well-paying assignment. She had the free time available and the money in her bank account to see her through several months. Dumb luck…or a nudge from fate?

"What's another hour?" Reid patted the bed and winked. In a booming, carnival-hawker type of voice, he said, "Come on over, Daisy Lennox! Test your narrating skills! Engage and impress your audience! See if you can win the storytelling battle of the year against the amazing, the fantastic, the one and only champion of all narration, Reid Foster!"

"Please, please, please, Aunt Daisy?" Megan begged. "Read to us!"

Sudden laughter bubbled in Daisy's chest, causing her to momentarily drop her guard. Reading to the girls would be nice, especially if doing so eased some of the discomfort with Erin. But…reading the same book with Reid would require her to get close to him.

Close enough that they were sure to touch.

Their thighs, probably, since she'd have to sit right next to him. Or their fingers, as they turned the pages. Touching him, in any way, didn't seem terribly conducive to her goals.

But growing closer to her family definitely was. "That sounds fun," she said. "Just be prepared to lose your title, Mr. Champion. Because I'll have you know—"

"I'm really tired," Erin interjected, her words barely audible. "And I want to take a nap. Could you please go to the living room to read the rest of the book, so I can sleep? Please?"

On his feet instantly, Reid placed the back of his hand on her forehead. "You don't seem to have a fever. Anything hurt?"

"Huh-uh," she said. "I'm just tired."

"Ah. Well, a nap it is, then." Reid kissed her on the cheek, helped settle her on the bed and said, "Remember, there's a chance I won't be here when you wake up. If that were to happen, your aunt will take care of you until I'm back."

"Can't someone else make the mountain safe? I...I don't want you to leave."

"They need me there, kiddo. My job is one of my responsibilities, just like school is for you. If I don't show up, that makes it harder on everyone else I work with. Make sense?"

Erin squeezed her eyes shut. "I suppose."

Reid selected a plush, purple stuffed bear from the shelf, which he then tucked into Erin's arms as he perched himself on the edge of her bed. "I'll always come back, though. That's a promise you can count on. You know that, right?"

Nodding slowly, Erin pulled the bear close to her in a tight clutch. "B-but *she* doesn't know how we do things," she whispered. "You know how we do things."

This was hard. Seeing her brother's child struggle had a sobering, cold-bucket-of-water effect on Daisy. She wanted to help. She wanted to find a solution. But she had nothing.

"Here's what I think," Reid said, his manner gentle. "You know how we do things, and it would be really great if you could give your aunt some coaching tips. How does that sound?"

"I can help, too," Megan declared. "I know how we do things around this place!"

"Yup, you do. Both of you can help." Reid tousled Erin's hair. "Can you do that for me, monkey? I would really appreciate knowing you and your sister have everything under control."

"I guess, but I...I'm really tired." Erin yawned an impressive, and decidedly exaggerated, yawn. "I might sleep until you're done saving the mountain, so then Megan would have to help."

"That's quite the long while. You're sure you're feeling okay?" Erin nodded in reply. Sighing, Reid said, "Then maybe we should talk about what has you this tired?"

When Erin didn't so much as squeak, Reid glanced at Daisy and mouthed the word *sorry,* as he jerked his jaw toward the door. Daisy nodded in understanding and returned to her prior decision. Erin might be willing to talk, but not while Daisy remained in the room.

"Hey, Megan," Daisy said brightly. "I have an idea. Let's go to the kitchen and search the cupboards for cookie-baking ingredients. Maybe chocolate chip or peanut butter?"

The younger Lennox daughter screwed up her face in contemplation. "I know! I want oatmeal cookies with butterscotch chips. They're Daddy's most favorite cookie ever and we can bring him some when we go see him. Can we? Please?"

At those words, a childhood memory slid into being. Daisy and Parker had baked those cookies with their mother every year on their father's birthday and on Father's Day. They weren't only Parker's favorite, they were Charles Lennox's first choice in cookies, as well.

It was a bittersweet remembrance.

"Oatmeal scotchies are delicious," Daisy said to Megan, who was watching her with rapt attention. "We just need to make sure we have the proper ingredients."

Megan twisted in a half circle and bounded from the bedroom, her enthusiasm almost contagious. They would have fun, she knew, and she looked forward to spending the time with Megan. She just wished Erin would join them.

"Cookies it is," Daisy said to Reid and Erin. "If either of you decide to put on your baker's hats, you'll know where to find us."

"Maybe we will at that," Reid said. "Give us a few minutes here."

Before Daisy could leave the room, Jinx plunked her butt on the carpet in a single-minded, I'm-not-moving position. She stared in the direction of Erin's bed and whined. Loudly.

And that was when inspiration struck.

Leaning over, she picked up Jinx and carried her directly to Erin, who was watching them with curiosity. "I think Jinx is sleepy and wants to rest with you, Erin. Would that be okay?"

The child's eyes rounded and her mask of distance softened, replaced by the same deep yearning that Daisy had witnessed earlier. "She wants to stay with me? Really and truly?"

Laughing at the dog's near-frantic attempts to leap onto the bed, Daisy said, "Oh, I'd say she definitely, really and truly, wants to stay with you. If you're good with the idea?"

"Yes." A small smile tipped Erin's lips upward. "Jinx can rest with me."

Warmth and a sweetness that Daisy had never before experienced expanded within. No, a nap with Jinx wouldn't solve the core problem—whatever that problem might be—but they had to start somewhere. And this was somewhere.

Moving closer to the bed—and therefore, closer to Reid—Daisy carefully set down Jinx. And her smart, smart dog pressed her body next to Erin's, laid her head on the girl's stomach, let out a contented-sounding huff and shut her eyes. Completely at peace.

Slowly, almost reverently, Erin stroked Jinx's neck and back. "She's so pretty," she said. "And…and I think she likes me." A wistful expression appeared. "Do you think she does?"

"I can guarantee that she likes you." An ounce of the pressure on Daisy's shoulders dissipated. "Maybe after your nap, I'll show you some of Jinx's favorite toys? She especially likes squeaky toys."

Erin continued to lightly rub Jinx. Daisy waited through the silence, hoping that the promise of spending additional time with Jinx would propel her niece to agree.

Thirty seconds, maybe a little less, elapsed before Erin said, "I guess so."

That small, simple answer raised Daisy's hopes to the next level. "Then we have a date."

She turned to leave when Reid grasped her wrist, his touch gentle. Warm and solid. "A date, is it?" he asked in that annoyingly rich tenor of his. Humor sparkled there, as well. "I have a date for you. May sixth. Might want to mark your calendar, Daisy."

Several sarcastic comebacks landed on the tip of her tongue, but Daisy swallowed every one of them in favor of a graceful exit. Tugging free, she exited the room with her head held high. Egging him on would serve no purpose.

Little chance existed that she would ever forget that date, marked calendar or not. That was the day, every year since the year she left, that she'd reflect. Wonder. Imagine what might have happened if she'd ignored her instincts, if she'd stayed, if she'd married Reid.

And every year, she reached the exact same conclusion. She would not—even if given the opportunity through some magical means—alter that particular decision. Yes, leaving had been more difficult than she could have imagined. Yes, Reid had once given her a sense of completeness, wholeness and security that she'd lacked on her own.

A sense so strong, so all-encompassing, that it had taken her far too long to find herself, to wake up each morning and not feel the loss of something—someone—essential, and she wouldn't, then or now, surrender what she'd worked so hard to attain.

Her independence. Not needing anyone else to feel alive or content or…real.

The kitchen resembled the snowy white appearance of the outdoors. Somehow, and Reid didn't exactly know how, Daisy and Megan had managed to coat the counters and a large portion of the tile floor in a fine layer of flour. Their hair, clothes and noses were dusted in white.

It was, he decided, quite the charming picture.

"How's Erin?" Daisy asked, noticing his arrival. "Is she doing any better?"

Erin hadn't, despite Reid's efforts, opened up about the cause of her anxiety. She insisted she was tired, nothing more. But he figured most of her unease had to do with facing yet another change in such short order. Time, in that case, would make the most difference.

"She is. Due in no small part to that ornery dog of yours." The creature had the audacity to growl at him when he kissed Erin on the cheek. One way or another, he and that dog would become friends. "We can talk more later, before I take off for the afternoon."

With a quick nod of understanding, Daisy slid a cookie-dough-filled sheet into the oven and started the timer. Megan stood on a chair and spooned glops of dough on another baking sheet, seemingly happy and comfortable with the same change that had so upset Erin.

Pushing aside his concerns for now, Reid said, "Seems the baking is going well." He took one full step into the kitchen, and before he could process the teasing grins Daisy and Megan exchanged or their flurry of movement, he was met with two handfuls of flour in the face…causing him to sneeze. Not just once, but twice.

Well, that answered the question of the indoor blizzard.

Wiping off his face with his sleeve, he gave the woman and the child the sternest, I'm-not-pleased expression he could form. Neither of them bought it. Megan just about dissolved into a state of hysterical, breath-stealing giggles, while Daisy contented herself with a knowing smirk aimed in his direction. He figured he had two choices.

One of which involved a kiss. The other involved retaliation.

Unfortunately, the kiss would have to wait until he and Daisy were alone. Retribution it was, then. Reid shrugged and, playing the you-got-me-good routine, walked toward the sink, saying, "How long were you two cookin' that one up?"

In between her giggles, Megan said, "It was all my idea! I got Aunt Daisy first, and then she got me, and then I got her again, and then I said we should get you."

"Oh, yeah?" In the second before he reached the sink, he pivoted, wrapped his arms around Megan's waist and hauled her up. Her giggles reached new proportions of hysteria. God, he hadn't heard her laugh like this since before Parker's accident. "Guess what, peanut?"

"Wh-what?"

Carrying her toward the open container of flour on the counter, he winked at Daisy. She grinned back. And he saw them—clear as day—several years down the road in their own home, with their own child, laughing and loving and living. *His* family.

The absolute rightness of this scene, of this potential reality, fused into Reid's DNA and became as permanent, as factual, as the dark brown shade of his eyes, the angled edge of his jaw…the strength and surety of his convictions. Some might call such a moment nothing more than déjà vu or groundless hope or…well, insanity.

Reid knew different. Such a moment could only be described as a gift.

A glimpse, he supposed, of what could have been. Of what could still be, if he played his cards right and everything aligned just so. Reinforcements couldn't hurt, though.

His family, in particular. Between Reid's two brothers, his sister and his parents—not to mention a pair of his siblings' significant others—he'd corral the support that a situation like this required. Soon, he'd arrange a meeting for the whole crew. They would be surprised by his intent, his plan, but they wouldn't let him down.

"Well, it's like this," he said to Megan, forcing his attention to the present. "You don't have near enough flour on your nose." Sitting the giggling girl on the counter, he dipped his fingers into the flour, which he then smeared on her nose. "Or your chin." He dabbed a dash of powder on her chin. "Or your cheeks. Or your—"

"Or your hair." Daisy slid into position on his left and reached into the container. Before he had the opportunity to react, she damn near dumped a fistful of flour on top of his head. The powder fell down his face, leaving him unable to see and sputtering white puffs into the air. "Why, look at that, Megan," Daisy said. "It seems we got to build a snowman today, after all."

Eyes bright with excitement, Megan gave her head a decisive shake. "Not yet, Aunt Daisy. His hair isn't white enough to look all the way like snow. I think he needs more."

"You do, huh?" Daisy reached around Reid, set to grab another handful.

Taking hold of her wrist, he tugged her toward him. He might not be able to kiss her, but he could certainly put the idea of a kiss into her mind. "I wouldn't do that if I were you," he said, keeping his voice steady and sure. Slowly, purposefully, he dropped his gaze to her mouth. "My methods of payback don't involve anything as simple as a bag of flour."

Like earlier, her tongue darted out to lick her lips. Like earlier, the minuscule motion jolted his body to full awareness. Of her. Of the many ways they could please each other.

Of the many ways they once had.

"Unfair," she whispered. "You don't get to make up your own rules. Not with this."

"When something this important is at stake, defining the rules is exactly what I get to do." Their gazes caught, held, and the heat between them became tangible. "Otherwise, I would be giving up without a fight. I already did that once, darlin'. I won't do so again."

"I don't have to accept your rules."

"Nope," he said, capitulating without argument. No reason not to when she spoke the truth. "But that will only inspire me to try harder. Increase my determination to succeed."

"It won't matter. Wouldn't have mattered then, either." One blink. Two blinks. "I don't regret my decision. You should know that now, before you take this nonsense any further."

Logically speaking, he'd long since assumed she'd found some version of peace, because she hadn't contacted him or reached out to make amends. Though, he supposed, he hadn't done so, either. But no remorse? Not one solitary wish to change any of what occurred?

That was a hard pill to swallow. Because Reid had plenty of both.

"You're telling me you have zero regrets?" he asked, directing all of his strength on shielding his shock. "None at all?"

"Not about the decision, no," she said, her voice catching slightly on the words, on the admittance. "I would make the same choice today."

The shock disappeared, replaced by pain. It slammed into him, and like a friggin' hacksaw, chewed through every muscle, every tendon, every cell and molecule, until the agony of her statement reverberated all the way through to his bones.

Hell, maybe it went as far as his soul.

"Without hesitation, Daisy?" he asked, his voice low.

"I…would have tried to talk with you, but yes. Without

hesitation," she said, each word ringing with pure, unrestricted honesty. "I enjoy my life, Reid. I like the person I have become far more than I liked the person I was. Think about that."

Oh, he would. For countless, sleepless hours, he was sure.

What he said, though, was "Well, I'd like the chance to get to know the person you've become. But, Daisy, I don't expect to stop lov—" All at once, he realized they were dipping into dangerous ground with a pint-size audience. Switching tacks, he winked at Megan, grabbed a large handful of flour and raised it above Daisy's head. As he opened his fist, he said, "I don't expect to stop loving…this look. White hair suits your aunt, don't you think, peanut?"

And in the wisdom only a child can have, Megan took in the scene and said, "When Erin and I don't get along, Daddy says we have to kiss and make up." She slid herself to the edge of the counter and jumped down. "You guys weren't getting along. So…kiss and make up."

"We're getting along just fine," Daisy said quickly. "We were just…talking."

"But we *were* in a disagreement, so technically speaking, I believe Megan is right." Reid stepped closer to Daisy and brushed some of the flour off her lips. "We really should make up. After all, whether Parker is here or not, his rules still apply."

"Yep!" Megan chimed in. "He wants us to be nice."

"Nice is one thing," Daisy said. "But technically speaking or not, I highly doubt my brother would expect us to—" The oven timer went off. Daisy blew out a breath, sending a cloud of white powder wafting around her. With a smug grin, she scooted to the side. "Well, there you have it. The cookies are done, so this conversation is over. We'll have to…make up later."

"Why would we want to do that?" Reid put himself in

front of her and draped his arm around her shoulders. One fast pull, and she was right there. Right where he wanted her. Her eyes widened, then narrowed. Her jaw clenched. And he figured he had five—maybe ten—seconds before her temper ignited and she slapped him. Nah, she'd kick him. "One kiss, Daisy. Just one."

Then, before she could put up a fuss, he kissed her. Not in the way he yearned to. Not in the way he would've if they were alone. But a kiss, nonetheless. Short and sweet, but real. And he felt the flicker of heat, the promise of more, in the meeting of their lips.

Just as he always had.

"That's silly!" Megan said. "Daddy doesn't mean we should really kiss, just that we should be nice and…and always remember that we love each other."

"Ah. I must have misunderstood. But still, that's real good advice, Megan," Reid said, keeping all of his attention on the woman he'd just kissed. "To be nice and always remember who we love. Don't you agree that's good advice, Daisy?"

"No regrets, Reid," she said, her voice firm. Her eyes, though, they weren't firm or hard or cold. They were warm and soft and…beautiful. "Remember that."

Oh, he would. But only for what it was. Painful information to absorb, yes, but also no more than a single, solitary component of the complete picture. A picture that contained many elements, including his hope. His belief. His unexplainable certainty at obtaining a future with Daisy. And, outweighing the rest, his love for her.

In Reid's mind, those were damn good enough reasons to continue on, to not give up, to go for the proverbial bucket of gold at the end of the rainbow. So that was what he would do. Without hesitation or…no, he couldn't state without fear.

That was fine. The thought of losing Daisy again *should* scare him.

If anything, the presence of fear validated his instincts, his convictions, and proved that he was fighting for something—someone—vital to him and to his life.

## Chapter Six

Partly due to the weather, partly due to the reality of settling in and learning her nieces' routines, more than a week passed before Daisy was able to take the girls to visit Parker. Within those days, Daisy had continually attempted to breach the distance between herself and Erin.

Unless Jinx was in the room or the topic of discussion, though, Erin kept to her oh-so-polite approach. Daisy hadn't decided what she thought of this. On one hand, how could she complain about a child remaining polite? On the other, this aloofness didn't offer any hint of the best way to proceed or help her understand the origin of the problem.

They were, for the time being, stuck on pause.

The same, in fact, could be said for Reid, whom she'd seen less of in the past week and a half than she had in her first twenty-fours in Steamboat Springs. His work schedule had been intense, requiring him to leave the house early and return late. He was not, however, too exhausted to forget about his love-and-marriage, we-are-not-done agenda.

There were the comments he'd toss her way, every one of them referring in some form or fashion to May sixth. There was that confident air he carried himself with whenever they were in the same room, and when the girls weren't paying attention, that annoying-but-freaking-sexy grin of his, typically followed up by that devilish wink.

Small indications, yes, but when added with the random save-the-date cards she'd discover tucked in odd places—such as in the book she was reading or the silverware drawer—she had no doubt that Reid Foster's focus toward *marrying* her had not altered in the slightest.

And he'd kissed her—okay, more of a peck, but still—in front of Megan, and had then whispered that, later, he'd do a better job of it. When they were alone.

So, no. He had not thrown in the towel.

"Are we almost there?" Megan's chipper voice interrupted Daisy's never-ending, tumbling circle of concerns. They'd awakened to a beautiful and clear Saturday morning, and were now on their way to the hospital. "Does Daddy know we're coming?"

"Yes and yes," Daisy responded. She'd phoned Parker before they'd left to make certain he was prepared for a visit. He was. "And he's very, very excited to see both of you."

From what she understood, the girls weren't able to visit their father right after the accident due to their ages and the scope of his injuries. Parker had required several surgeries almost immediately, and hadn't been aware enough to interact with anyone for longer than a few minutes. Neither Parker nor Reid wanted to upset the girls with that visual reality, so they'd held off. The storm, of course, had caused another delay.

Now, though, the girls needed to see their dad.

"He's really going to be okay?" Erin's worry-laden voice brought forth a well of emotion. "When my mommy was sick, we went to the hospital to…to say goodbye. And Reid said that y-you might take care of us if D-Daddy died. I d-don't want to tell Daddy g-goodbye."

Megan instantly began to cry, and Erin followed suit.

Spying a convenience store to her right, Daisy flipped on her turn signal and yanked the car into the parking lot. No wonder Erin had seemed to dislike her on sight. She'd taken Daisy's surprise arrival as a sign her father was dying. And obviously, Reid had no idea he'd put that thought into Erin's head.

Once Daisy had the car stopped, she unbuckled her seat belt and pivoted. Both girls were sobbing. Megan's cries were louder, more vehement than the silent tears coursing down Erin's face. Didn't matter. Noisy or quiet, each were heartbreaking.

"This is not the same. Your father is still hurt, yes, but he is getting better. And the only reason I'm here is to help look after you until he can come home. Look at me, girls," Daisy said when neither Erin's nor Megan's tears subsided. "This is not a goodbye visit. This is a hello, we've-missed-you, we-love-you and we're-so-happy-to-see-you visit."

Erin's light brown eyes, just a shade darker than her sister's, watery and filled with fear, focused on Daisy. "Do you promise, Aunt Daisy? With your heart crossed and everything?"

"I promise. With my heart crossed and everything." Because she couldn't stand not to be closer to them in that second, Daisy climbed into the backseat. "I will never lie to either one of you. No matter what the question is, I will tell you the truth. Okay?"

"I can ask you anything, ever, and you'll never fib?" Erin asked, her curiosity at such a concept overruling her fear. "Always and forever?"

"Yes. Do you believe me?"

Erin studied her for a few seconds before dropping her chin in a jerky nod. She tightened her hold on her stuffed animal—the same purple bear Reid had handed her in her room that day—and said, "I won't fib to you, either. If you ask me something."

"Me, too, Aunt Daisy," Megan said. "No fibbing ever!"

"Well, then I'd say we have the start of a wonderful relationship." Daisy reached for and squeezed each of the girls' hands. "Ready to go see your dad now?"

The answer was, of course, a resounding yes.

Twenty minutes later, Daisy and her nieces stopped outside of Parker's room. Reid had already warned her and the girls what to expect when they saw him, but she thought a quick reminder might be smart. She kneeled down in front of them. "Remember what Reid said. Your daddy has some cuts and bruises. There will be machines near him that beep and make funny noises, but they're nothing to worry about. Okay?"

While Megan nodded immediately, Erin didn't. She opened her mouth, hesitated, and then as if recalling Daisy's promise, closed it again and also nodded.

Headway, perhaps? "Good. And if you have any questions, just ask."

Ignoring her jumpy stomach and her own bolt of fear over seeing her brother for the first time in so long, Daisy led the girls inside. Parker was half sitting on the bed, one leg hoisted above his body in some type of an uncomfortable-appearing mechanical contraption, and the other straight in front of him. Mottled bruises were on his arms—one of which was in a cast—his hands and his face. Beneath the injuries, he looked sturdier, more solid, than Daisy had expected. He was still her strong, confident older brother with the same sandy blond hair and friendly warmth emanating from his blue eyes. Some of her tension eased.

She'd missed him. More than she'd realized.

"Daddy!" both girls yelled at once. Neither moved forward, though. They were, Daisy assumed, caught in a web of longing and caution.

"Now there's the sight I've been waiting for," Parker said,

his pleasure and relief apparent. "Wow, have I missed you two. Come over here for a hug. I promise I won't break."

Erin made the first move, scooting to the edge of the bed. Carefully, as if truly concerned she could break her father, she eased in for a gentle hug. That was all it took for Megan to dash forward and propel herself into Parker's unencumbered, waiting arm. Parker began asking them questions about the past few weeks, and the girls happily answered.

As her nieces became reacquainted with their father, Daisy collapsed onto one of the guest chairs and released a pent-up breath. There were so many questions to ask Parker, so many possible topics they should—at some point— discuss, but she knew this wasn't the time.

They would need privacy, and perhaps, several easier-to-manage conversations first. So they could create a base-line, a new start to their relationship.

A sudden absence of noise drew her attention to the bed. Megan had crawled into position next to her father, while Erin had remained standing with her hand tightly clasped in Parker's. And her brother's contented expression, his absolute peace in this moment, reminded her again of all the time they'd wasted.

Family. *Her* family.

How stupid to forget—pretend?—that this connection no longer mattered, no longer held any weight or importance. What could be more important than family?

No, this wasn't the time to bring up past hurts or ask for Parker's input on Erin, or pose any of the questions that Daisy had wondered about for so long. They'd get there. She hoped they'd get there. Today was about…connecting. For the girls, for Parker. Maybe for herself, too.

"Hey there, big brother," she said when Parker's quiet, searching gaze finally landed on her. She forced her mouth into a teasing grin. "The mountain kicked your butt good, huh?"

"If you think this looks bad, you should see the mountain," Parker responded with his typical dry humor. "Fairly sure I managed to… Oh, who am I kidding? Yeah, the mountain kicked my butt. Did…ah…Reid mention he's the one who found me?" Now her brother's voice no longer held humor of any kind. "He stayed with me until transport could get me here, kept me talking and… Not sure where I'd be if it wasn't for him."

Gratitude and relief sank in fast. "No, he didn't mention he'd saved your life." Emotion, heavy and hard, settled in the pit of Daisy's stomach. "Though, I suppose that's just like Reid, isn't it? He isn't the type of man to—"

"Blow his own horn," Parker said, completing Daisy's sentence. "And nope, he isn't. Never has been. But I thought you should know."

"I… Yes, I should know that." She considered, briefly, telling Parker about Reid's wedding mandate, but decided not to. The girls were, after all, within listening distance. Later, she'd thank Reid. She might even kiss… No, a hug would serve well enough.

"Don't think I'll be skiing for a long, long time." Parker rested his jaw on top of Megan's head and squeezed Erin's hand. "If ever again."

"But you've always loved to ski," she said, her thoughts still on Reid. "And you know what they say—when you fall off a horse, the best thing you can do is get right back on."

"There are some things I love more than skiing."

"I understand. I'm just so glad that you're…" She let her words die off, not wanting to cause the girls any additional concern. "And I'm also glad I'm here."

"Me, too." He closed his eyes for a beat. "Very much so…on both accounts. And I'm looking forward to going home."

"I bet."

"Will be a while, I think," Parker said. "A month at the

soonest, from what the doctor says. If I don't—" He glanced at his daughters. "One more...procedure needs to happen first, and then physical therapy. Can you...I mean, will you be able to stay for that long?"

"Yes," she answered, mentally working out the logistics. Living in Los Angeles didn't come cheap, but she was careful with her money. She could manage a couple of months without issue. And, well, if her brother needed her for longer than that, she'd find a way to make it happen. "I'll figure it out, Parker."

"Thank you," her brother said. "I want the girls to know you better."

"I would like that," she said. "Things...should be different between us."

From there, the conversation changed tempo. In mutual but silent accordance, Daisy and Parker kept the mood upbeat and cheerful. Bit by bit, the girls became chattier, slowly morphing into the children they probably were before their father's accident. And, other than their natural hesitation when the visit came to an end, they remained talkative during the drive home.

"Aunt Daisy?" Erin asked from the backseat. "Can we all build snowmen after lunch? I...I want to try something special."

"Absolutely." Smiling, Daisy pulled into the house's driveway and shut off the ignition. "I think that sounds like a great plan. Perfect, actually."

The girls exploded from the car and raced toward the front door. Daisy sat still for a minute, allowing herself to savor the joy of this moment. Yes, everything would be okay. Yes, she was supposed to be in Steamboat Springs.

Not forever, no. But for now, there was nowhere else she'd rather be.

Saturday afternoon found Reid walking into Foster's Pub and Grill—one of the two local businesses his family owned and operated—with knotted nerves and tense muscles. He might have chosen to bring his family onboard, but that didn't negate his anxiety in the disclosure.

He had not a doubt that each of the Fosters would stand behind him in solidarity, but they would also be protective. They, of course, weren't aware that Reid might have been able to minimize the damage. Not only for Daisy, but also for himself. And he wouldn't share the details of the secret he'd kept today. Couldn't, really, when he hadn't yet told Daisy.

Reid stopped inside the wide double doors and appraised the room. While the pub's lunchtime rush had ended, plenty of folks still sat at the well-polished oak bar and the round, also oak, tables. Funny to think that in another week—two, tops—the city would begin to grow increasingly silent as the winter tourist season crawled to a close.

Nodding toward a few of the pub's regulars, Reid made his way to the kitchen at the rear of the building. He'd phoned his mother yesterday, had asked her to gather everyone together this afternoon. Margaret Foster had agreed without question or comment, though he figured she had plenty of both. Especially if she'd caught wind of Daisy's return.

Even if she hadn't, she—along with everyone else—would be mighty curious about his request. The Fosters typically held their business meetings in the middle of each month, so the March gathering wasn't scheduled for another week or so. And since these meetings—which were just as much social as they were business-oriented—tended to be held after hours, asking for everyone to find time in the midst of their busy day was unprecedented.

Waving at a few of the employees, he wound through the kitchen to the stairs that led to the now vacant apartment above the restaurant. All of the Foster siblings had lived there at one time or another, the most recent being his sister, Haley.

When she'd moved out, their parents had decided to turn the apartment into a large office area, complete with a conference table. And that was where today's meeting was set to take place. Reid paused at the top of the stairs and inhaled a calming breath. Stupid as all get-out to be so nervous. This was his family. He could count on them.

The truth of that thought steeled his resolve, so he opened the door to let himself in. And quickly saw that everyone had already arrived. Early, even, by a good fifteen minutes.

"Guess I made you all rather curious, huh?" he asked, walking directly to the table where everyone was seated. "Because I can't remember us ever starting on time for anything."

Haley grinned in apparent good humor, but Reid didn't miss the concern glimmering in her sage-green eyes. Her other half, Gavin—who stood close to six foot five and had a build resembling a linebacker's—sat beside her with a fair portion of worry in his own gaze. Glancing around the table, Reid recognized the same in every last member of his family.

Hell. He'd caused them stress. And that had not been his goal.

"Let me say this straight-out," he said, taking the empty chair next to his brother Dylan. "I'm not sick or moving away or becoming a monk. I don't have bad news to share. So whatever you all think is going on, chances are you're wrong."

"Good to hear," said Paul Foster, the patriarch of the family. He turned to his wife, who sat beside him, and patted her hand. "Your mother has been coming up with all sorts of outlandish ideas to explain why you might have requested this get-together."

Reid nodded but didn't reply. Looking at his dad was a lot like seeing a future version of himself. Reid and his brother Cole took after Paul the most in appearance, with the same black hair and dark eyes. Haley and Dylan more closely resembled their mother, with their reddish-brown hair and their chameleon—sometimes brown, sometimes green—eyes.

All of the Foster kids shared the long, lean frames of their father, and fortunately, the same high-powered metabolism that allowed them to eat whenever, whatever they wanted.

Pushing a long strand of hair behind her ear, Haley leaned forward. "Is someone pregnant? Am I going to be an aunt?"

"Nope," Reid said, chuckling. "No babies just yet."

"Hmm. My guess was monk," said Cole, the youngest of the brothers, with a wink in Reid's direction. "But you already ruled that one out, so I have no idea what's up."

One by one, the rest of the Fosters tossed in a selection of notions, some harebrained and some not. Resigned, Reid watched, listened and stayed silent. When his family got going, the best you could do was sit tight and keep your mouth shut until a lull presented itself.

When one did, he coughed to clear his throat. No reason to beat around the bush, so he dived right in, saying, "Daisy's in town, due to Parker's accident. She showed up the week before last, on a Tuesday night, and I…ah…hadn't known she was coming."

"Daisy's back?" Dylan shook his head as if the entire idea perplexed him. "Why… I mean, is she here to stay?"

"That was…*ten* full days ago!" Haley said. "Just like you to keep this news to yourself for so long. Geez, Reid. Why would… Oh. Has Parker taken a turn for the worse?"

"No, Parker's doing well. Daisy's here to temporarily help with the girls." And then, since Cole was attempting to whisper an explanation to his blond-haired, blue-eyed fiancée, Rachel, Reid said, "Daisy is the woman I almost married, Rach. I'm not sure if you remember her from when we were all kids or if you know what took place. If not, Cole can fill you in."

"I remember her, and I've heard a little," Rachel said, her voice quiet. "And wow, Reid, that must have been a shock for you, seeing her out of the blue."

*A shock, yes, and a whole lot more.* "It's been...interesting."

"How is Daisy?" Margaret asked. "And more to the point, how are you?"

"Daisy is fine. She—" Reid wanted to get to the heart of the matter, let his family absorb the information, and then return to Parker's house. So, without further ado, he said, "I still love her. And I've decided to plan another wedding and hope she chooses to attend."

An invisible tremor rocked the room at his announcement, silencing everyone. His mother closed her eyes and his father's eyebrows drew together in worry.

"Wait, wait, wait," Dylan said, breaking the quiet. "Let me get this straight. You've *decided* to plan another wedding and you *hope* she'll attend? I take that as meaning—"

"At this juncture, she has flat-out said no." Reid stretched his legs in front of him and tried for a casual, confident pose. "I plan on changing her mind, but I could use some help from all of you. Which is why we're here."

"So now," Cole said, focusing on Reid, his voice neither condemning nor accepting, "you're the one attempting to get the girl you love by means of...what would you call this? Trickery or game-playing or...hell, I don't know. What's your definition?"

"Neither. I'm not tricking Daisy, nor am I playing a game." In an effort to win Rachel's affections, Cole *had* resorted to a game of subterfuge. Reid had not approved.

"I've made my intent and feelings clear. She is well aware that I want to marry her. We've even set a date."

"Taking this a little far a little fast, aren't you?" Reid's father asked. "And why would Daisy set a date if she hasn't accepted your proposal?"

"Too far? No. Too fast?" Reid shrugged. "Probably, but I don't have a lot of time to waste. And I don't know why she chose a date, but she did." He tucked his hands behind his head. "I've decided to take that as a positive sign I'm heading in the proper direction."

Gavin chuckled half under his breath. "Or she couldn't stand up to the force of a Foster's will." He winked at Haley. "I know something about how that goes."

Haley snorted. "If I hadn't shown you the force of my will, you'd be hiding out in that house of yours, pretending you were happy without me. And we both know—"

"Wait. Everyone, just wait," Dylan said again. Tipping backward in his chair, he frowned at Reid. "I can't wrap my head around this. Why would you decide to marry a woman who has already proven she's unable to commit? Seems as if you're just asking for trouble."

Like Reid, Dylan had once lost the woman he loved. He'd married almost directly out of high school, and his wife had gone and fallen for someone else. Within a year of marriage, they were filing for divorce. Therefore, Reid was not surprised to hear this question from Dylan.

"I might be." He shrugged again. "Won't stop me, though."

"You're really this sure?"

"Yup. Can't explain it, really. It's this pure, absolute type of knowledge that stems from somewhere other than my brain. I love Daisy. And this time, I can't let her go without trying."

Resting her cheek on Gavin's shoulder, Haley sighed.

Of all of his siblings, Reid had figured his sister would come around first. She was chock-full of romantic notions.

"I'm on your side," she said, confirming this belief. "Whatever you need, I'll do."

"Me, too," Cole said. "I know where you're at right now. And…yeah, whatever you need. Just as Haley said. All you have to do is point me in the right direction."

Rachel murmured her agreement, as well, followed by Gavin. His parents and Dylan remained stoic in their silent regard. Still concerned, he wagered.

He started with his folks. "What are you two thinking?"

Margaret laced together her fingers and leveled her shoulders. "I don't know about your dad, but I'm thinking of those days after Daisy left. I'm remembering your devastation, Reid, and how long it took you to regain your footing. I don't…I just don't know if this—"

"Makes a lick of sense," Paul interjected. "Each of you kids have come up with one harebrained scheme after another. No wonder my hair is turning gray."

"They have, yes, but in the name of love," Margaret said softly. "I can't find fault in choosing love, even with my concerns."

"Um. Not me," Dylan said. "No harebrained schemes coming from this direction. In the name of love or not. Single. Staying so, too."

"Just wait until the day the perfect woman walks in your path," Haley said. "You'll change your tune soon enough."

"I most certainly will not."

Cole snickered. On another day, in another moment, Reid would've joined in with the teasing. Not today and not in this moment.

When the room quieted again, Paul said, "Like your mother, I remember the fallout, son. So I have to ask… have you two had an honest conversation about what happened back then? Do you believe—assuming Daisy agrees to your unique proposal and then manages to arrive for the wedding this time—that the two of you can create a stable relationship?"

"I'm as sure as I can be, but no, we haven't entered into a discussion about our history as of yet. We will, though. And, Mom, I won't lie. If this doesn't pan out the way I hope, I will be…upset. No way around that one." A lump the size of Texas manifested in Reid's throat. "However, I will be far worse off if I don't give this—me and Daisy—a go. That's just the way it is, so I'm asking for your trust and support."

Paul and Margaret exchanged a look that was decipherable only to them, and then, with slight shrugs and weary expressions, they both nodded. "If you're certain, then we're here for you," Paul said. "Just proceed with caution and preparation for a…less-than-ideal outcome."

"And of course, we trust you. You always have our support. But that doesn't mean I can snap my fingers and forget the pain that Daisy brought you," Margaret said. "If she doesn't purposely cause you additional pain, I can…well, I *think* I can forgive. I'll do my best."

His mother. So fierce, so loyal. He'd love her regardless, but he loved her, respected her, even more for those qualities.

"None of this is that simple." Reid selected his words carefully, thoughtfully. "There are details about what happened that you aren't aware of, and I'm not at liberty to tell you what they are right now. My history with Daisy isn't as clear-cut as you might think."

"I suppose that's fair." A brief pause and then the hint of a smile appeared. "It seems we have a wedding to plan. When…what's the date?"

"May sixth."

Margaret gasped. "The same date?"

"Yup." He didn't offer any additional clarification. No

reason to. "We're starting from square one, so basically everything from the ceremony to the reception needs to be worked out. All I ask is that no one mentions my house to Daisy, not even a hint of where I live."

Another secret that Daisy did not know was that, shortly before their original wedding date, he'd bought the house she'd adored as a girl. Her gingerbread house, a place she'd believed fairies had lived. It was meant to be a surprise, and well, he'd never considered living elsewhere. A sign he should've paid attention to long before now.

"Hold on here," Dylan said. "Don't get me wrong, I'm in. I'll help. But before we start digging into this—to use Dad's words—harebrained scheme, I have another question."

"Go for it. What's up?"

"You love the girl. Fine," Dylan said. "But does the girl love you?"

"I believe she does, though I don't know for sure," Reid admitted, again unsurprised by Dylan's forthrightness. "For now, let's proceed with the theory that she does. Or will again."

Though, even if Daisy's love hadn't died or could be resurrected, she might not forgive him when she learned the truth. That, Reid knew, was where his deepest fear resided. When she discovered that he could've saved her from that wedding-morning confessional-from-hell, chances were high she wouldn't require any other reason to walk away from the second-chance-at-forever wish she'd written in her letter.

He couldn't avoid the truth. Wouldn't choose anything other than honesty this go-round. Once he'd found the right time and place, he'd man up and do what he should've done before.

"Reid?" Haley's voice yanked Reid clean from his thoughts. "Are we planning a casual or a formal wedding? And what about the ceremony location? Or the reception? Or—"

"Let's keep it simple," he said. "Daisy would like it simple." Another thought came to him, so he turned toward Cole and Rachel. "I'm sorry about jumping in and stealing your wedding-day thunder. If I'd seen this coming, I would've warned you."

"Nothing to apologize for. Rach and I will be married and back from our honeymoon by May sixth," Cole replied with an easy, relaxed air. "And our wedding is set to go. Rachel's been a freak of nature in that regard. Compulsively organized, why you wouldn't believe—"

Rachel lightly punched Cole on his forearm. "And aren't you glad of that now? Other than final fittings and confirmations, we're done." She smiled at Reid. "So we have plenty of hands-on experience to offer."

"Thanks, guys," Reid said. "It's appreciated."

"May sixth, huh? So…nine-ish weeks from now?" Haley dug through her purse and pulled out a notepad and pen. "Let's do this! We need two lists. One for the actual details of the wedding, and another for helping Reid convince Daisy to…well, not abandon ship."

Everyone began talking at once, bringing up possibilities and ideas. This time, though, Reid joined in the conversation, secure in the knowledge that if this whole kit-and-caboodle went south, he had his family's support. Which was a relieving concept.

What this knowledge didn't do was make the haunting prospect of losing Daisy a second time any less of a weight to carry. Hell. It seemed that Dylan had perfectly and concisely summed up Reid's predicament. He was, in effect, just asking for trouble.

## Chapter Seven

By the time Reid left the pub, almost two hours had passed. He was pleased with the afternoon's progress. Together, he and his family had conceived of a plan to keep the wedding wheels turning. Nothing outlandish. Nothing that involved trickery or subterfuge.

Mostly, they'd focused on simple reinforcement. Whether that would be enough or not remained to be seen, but he wasn't in this alone. That, all on its own, made a world of difference.

Reid first stopped at the hospital to see Parker, but his friend was sound asleep, so he'd gone home to retrieve a few necessary items. In particular, Daisy's engagement ring, which he'd never found the will to sell, trash or hurl from the top of the mountain. Once he had the ring in his possession, he returned to the road, whistling as he drove.

Not so much in optimism as in certainty of the path he'd chosen.

When he pulled his SUV into Parker's driveway, behind Daisy's car, it was to the sight of two lopsided snowmen, the beginnings of a third and…a snow dog?

Daisy and the girls were focused on completing the third snowman, and Erin and Megan were dressed appropriately for the cold weather. Jinx, he noted in some humor, wore a fuzzy, hot-pink canine sweater. But Daisy? She had on that blasted spring jacket, sneakers and—while he couldn't say for certain from his driver's seat vantage point—what looked to be neon orange socks masquerading as a pair of gloves.

In other words, she was all but begging for pneumonia.

Before his logical brain had a chance to function, he'd jumped from the vehicle and was storming toward Miss Sunny California. His irritation and concern at her seeming inability to…to…take care of herself becoming larger, more intense, with each step. She'd grown up in Colorado, hadn't she? Yup, she had. And that meant she knew better.

Fortunately, the sound of Erin's and Megan's happy giggles pushed in past his emotional stew, forcing him to stop midstride. Forcing him to rethink his approach.

Lecturing Daisy at all, but especially in witness of the girls, wouldn't earn him any points in the romance department. Besides which, whether she seemed so at this particular moment or not, Daisy was an adult. If she chose to risk illness by prancing in the freezing cold weather while attired in unsuitable outerwear, he supposed that was her call to make.

Not the smartest call, but hers.

And if she came down with a cold, he'd make her chicken noodle soup and hot tea and he'd…he'd take care of her. Whether she damn well liked it or not.

For now, though, he set his worry on the back burner, formed his mouth into a smile and relaxed his posture. "What do we have going on here?" he asked, approaching the group of adorably pink-cheeked females. "And why wasn't I invited?"

"You're invited, Reid!" Megan said, lurching toward him for a hug. "Look! We made a snowman for each of us, even Jinx. And when we go inside, we're going to have hot chocolate and cookies and watch a movie. And Aunt Daisy said we'll have pizza for dinner! But first—"

"Wow. Hot chocolate, cookies and pizza, all in the same day?"

"Pepperoni pizza," Erin said as she patted the head of the snowman into a less lopsided shape. "But Aunt Daisy says we have to eat salad with dinner."

"No way! She said we have to eat salad?" Then, ignoring Daisy's flustered scowl and amidst the girls' bubbling laughter, Reid pretended to give the snowmen a slow, in-depth once-over. "I see Daisy's snowman, and Erin's and Megan's. I see Jinx's, too. But—" he scratched his jaw and stepped backward and searched the yard "—where's my snowman?"

"We waited for you." Daisy stuck her sock-covered hands in her jacket pockets and shivered. "Due to the rules of snow magic."

"Snow magic?" Reid said. "Uh…should I ask?"

"Aunt Daisy didn't know this, but I thought you would," Erin said, sounding somewhat flabbergasted. "If you want any snow magic in your snowman—"

"You have to start each of the snowballs yourself," Megan explained, her voice rising a pitch as she spoke. "With your own two hands."

"Uh-huh. We can help with the rest of the snowman, just not the start. That part was hard with Jinx," Erin explained. "We had to use her paws to smush the snow into small balls."

"And all of our snowmen have to be built on the same day, so you have to do yours now. Not tomorrow." Megan gave Reid a very stern look. "Or our snow magic might not work, and…and it *has* to work. So Daddy can come home soon."

In a soft, quiet voice, Erin added, "We might need some magic for that."

Aha. Reid didn't know where the notion of snow magic originated from, but it didn't take a rocket scientist to understand the heartfelt seriousness of the request.

"So you can see how important this is," Daisy said, her eyes bright from the cold. Also, Reid guessed, from emotion. "Besides, who wouldn't want some snow magic in their life?"

"I absolutely want—" Reid snapped his jaw shut as Jinx suddenly dove for his ankles with a whine-growl-yowl noise. Unbeknownst to Daisy, he'd spent the past few nights trying to warm up to her paranoid pooch. Obviously, he'd been less than successful. "Daisy?" he asked as Jinx dug her teeth into his jeans. "Can you…?"

"Can I…what?"

"Really?" When she didn't respond, he pointed at the dog attached to his body. "I'm not going to be able to build a snowman, magical or otherwise, with your dog yapping at my ankles."

"Of course." Daisy came forward and unlatched her dog from his pant leg. Picking up the unruly creature, she said, "But if you'll recall, I warned you right off that she won't stop so long as you're here. And, if you'll also recall, you said that you were fairly certain you could outwait a dog. Guess you were wrong on that account, huh?"

"Oh, I can outwait Jinx," he answered. "I can outwait just about anyone or anything if the need arises. Even, in case you're wondering, a reluctant bride. However, you and—"

"You think I'm *reluctant?*"

*"However,"* he repeated, "you and the girls are cold. I would prefer to get all three of you inside sooner rather than later. Before that can happen, I need to build a magic snowman. But yes, Daisy, I believe you're understandably reluctant. Luckily, I'm a patient man."

"Obstinate, not patient. And here I was, feeling all warm

and gracious toward you, and then you…you have to ruin it!" Speaking in a lower volume, she said, "Thank you. For saving my brother's life. For…being there for him when I was not. I…just thank you, so much."

"You're welcome. It's… Well, I'm just glad I was there." Then, due to his discomfort at receiving attention of that sort, he grinned. "You know, I was thinking we could just drive to Vegas and skip the rest of the hoopla altogether. What do you think?"

Exasperation, quick and vivid, entered her expression and colored her cheeks a deeper shade of pink. "What you want," she said, keeping her voice low, so only he could hear, "is not happening. I keep hoping you'll come to your senses, but apparently, you have an obvious issue with admitting you're in error."

"That's a no on Vegas, huh?"

"You need to accept defeat, Reid."

"Sorry, that's something I just cannot do."

She opened her mouth—ready to light into him, he was sure—glanced at the girls' earnest expressions and promptly clamped her lips shut. Giving her head a quick shake, she said, "You're right. Everyone is cold, so I'll take Jinx inside and start the hot cocoa. But we're not done with this conversation."

"Nope, we're not," he agreed. "We have a lot of decisions to make before May sixth. Probably a smart idea to start those discussions soon."

Her mouth thinned in frustration but she remained silent. Tossing one last glare in his direction, she whipped around and stomped toward the house. Jinx, not to be outdone, offered a series of rumbling growls and short, yippy barks as she was carried off.

It was, Reid decided, a rather humorous scene.

The second the *reluctant* love of his life disappeared through the front door, Reid focused all of his attention on

Erin and Megan, saying, "We have several things to talk about, but first…tell me about this snow magic. Where did you hear about it and how does it work?"

"It's from a story," Erin explained. "If we all build our snowmen while thinking of one great wish—has to be the same wish for all of us, though, 'cause that makes the magic stronger—then at night, the snow fairies will sprinkle magic dust on the snowmen and our wish will come true. So our wish is for Daddy to be able to come home. Soon."

"But we have to think about the wish the whole time we're making your snowman," Megan said. "Or the fairies won't hear our wishing."

"And just because it's from a story doesn't mean it isn't true," Erin said, lifting her chin in that familiar stubborn way. "I asked Aunt Daisy, because she promised she'd never fib to us. Ever. And she said she couldn't say if there was snow magic or not, but that if we believed really, really hard, anything can happen."

"So we're believing really, really hard," Megan said, blinking several times in quick succession. "Really, really, *really* hard! For Daddy."

There wasn't a man on the face of the earth who could argue with the possibility of snow magic under such circumstances. "I think the same…that if you truly believe, anything at all can happen." Reid held out his arms and both girls piled in. Once they separated, he said, "Let's build this snowman. For your dad."

And so they did.

Inch by delicious inch, Daisy submerged her body into the hot bubble bath and sighed in relief when the water met her chin. Pushing a stray wisp of hair from her cheek, she let the warmth soak in, taking pleasure from the humble reality of no longer shivering.

March in Steamboat Springs could remain wickedly

cold, and today's romp in the snow had frozen her clear through. Even spending the rest of the day indoors hadn't erased the chill. Her hands and feet were chapped, her cheeks and lips were windburned, she had the beginnings of a headache and…and…all of it was worth the fun she'd enjoyed with her nieces.

Now that she and Erin had reached an understanding, Daisy believed their connection would continue to grow. Slowly, yes. But steadily.

Daisy cupped her hands and filled them with the honeysuckle-scented bubbles. Pursing her lips, she blew gently, sending a spray of foam fluttering into the air. She didn't give herself many indulgences in her current life, but bubble baths were—in a word—*heavenly*.

Her version of self-therapy combined with sheer relaxation and utter peace.

Resting her weight against the cool porcelain of the clawfoot tub, Daisy's lashes drifted shut. Tight muscles loosened and the slight, throbbing pain in her temples dissipated.

Her breathing deepened. Sleepily, a vision of Reid came to her. Beneath her closed eyelids, she could see him, his arms around her. Loving her. Misty water stroked along the length of her body, as she imagined what he would do, caressing her skin with its silky warmth.

With a long, drawn-out exhale of desire, Daisy feathered her fingertips from the flatness of her belly to the curves of her breasts, envisioning the trail Reid would take if it were his hands on her. A soft, barely heard moan slipped from her throat as she delved deeper into her private fantasy world. What would he do next? Knowing Reid, he'd kiss her. Fully, soundly.

She moved her fingers to her lips. Yes, he would definitely kiss her. Then he'd—

*No, no, no.* Jerking open her eyes, Daisy sat up straight, the suddenness of her movement sloshing sudsy water over the edge of the tub. What was wrong with her? Why was she thinking—*fantasizing*—about having sex with Reid? Not smart. Not smart in any way.

Her heart knocked against her breastbone in a too-fast, too-hard rhythm. So much so, she felt the pressure of the beat in her ears. Wanting Reid, desiring Reid, would lead her to possibly *loving* Reid, and along that path lay…disaster.

Never again would she lose even one piece of her identity to a man. *Any* man.

The bathwater suddenly became icy and uncomfortable against her flushed skin. Yanking the plug, she watched as the water noisily gurgled down the drain. From here on out, for the next little while, she was a shower-only gal. Cold showers, at that.

She then attempted to remove every last thought of ever again becoming intimate with Reid from her brain and stepped from the tub. She dried off, slipped on a pair of pajama bottoms and a T-shirt and then waited until she'd regained control.

The girls were in bed for the night, emotionally exhausted after their visit with Parker and physically so from the hours of outdoor play. Megan's eyelids had started drooping in the middle of her first slice of pizza, and Erin's yawning hadn't been far behind.

Reid was awake, though. And unlike the past week, he hadn't spent the entirety of the day working. Which meant he'd be alert and ready for action. If she walked downstairs with her body tingling from the mere *remembrance* of his touch, and he somehow clued in to this mental state of being, she couldn't guarantee…a damn thing.

Not what she would say or how she would feel. Not how she would react. And God help her if he decided that tonight was the night to make good on his promise to kiss her… really kiss her. If he did, she might as well start shopping for her wedding gown now.

So, yeah, she waited. For a good long while.

When her balance returned and with her sanity in check, she left the bathroom and slowly took the stairs. She had a plan now. Not the greatest plan, but one that should get her through the rest of the evening. She'd stretch out on the couch with a book and, no matter what Reid might say or do, she'd keep her face buried in said book.

Oh, she likely wouldn't be able to focus on the words, but the physical form of the book should serve well enough as a shield. Maybe enough of a shield that Reid would decide to call it an early night and go to bed. Without her, of course.

At the foot of the stairs, she heard his voice coming from the kitchen. She would've assumed he was on the phone except for the cajoling sound of his tone mixed in with the recognizable rumbling of Jinx's growling.

Ha. He was trying to make nice with her dog, was he? As if none of her male friends had already attempted the same…and failed. It was, she knew, a losing proposition.

Smirking, Daisy quietly walked to the end of the hall-way and peered into the kitchen. Man and dog were at a standoff. Or, perhaps more accurate in this situation, a sit-off. Reid sat on the tile floor on one side of the room with a slice of deli meat—ham, she thought—dangling from his fingertips, while Jinx sat on the other side, her head held high in defiance.

Reid murmured persuasive words of encouragement. Jinx growled or whined—or both—in return. Her front legs trembled every so often, and her gaze remained frozen on the temptation in Reid's grasp. Easy to see that the poor dog desperately wanted the treat.

She just didn't want to have to cozy up to a man.

It didn't escape Daisy; the similarity of what had happened upstairs with what was occurring now. Only, she wasn't a dog and Reid wasn't a slice of ham. And the treat she yearned for came with a host of issues if she capitulated. Jinx would just make a new friend.

Mentally shaking the absurd comparison from her thoughts, Daisy back-stepped away from the kitchen and into the living room, where she retrieved her book from her suitcase, curled up on the couch and pretended to read. Her shield visibly in place.

Too bad she couldn't shield her heart with the same effectiveness.

Reid stared at Jinx in varying degrees of frustration and amusement. Yet another night of failure. Nothing he'd tried so far—squeaky toys, tennis balls, a chunk of rawhide or a friggin' piece of ham—had done the trick. The obstinate creature refused to let go of her disdain long enough to give him an opening. And he refused to give up trying.

His initial goal in becoming friends with Jinx was to prove to Daisy that he could. He'd gotten it into his head that if he were the man who managed to soften her dog's male-hating tendencies, her defenses toward him would relax some, as well. A dumb idea? Probably.

Somewhere along the line, though, his goal had shifted gears. He liked Jinx, and he disliked that she viewed him as a threat. And her behavior with him differed so greatly from her behavior with Daisy and the girls—all of whom she followed around as if they were covered in bacon grease—that he'd pretty much decided that some jerk had mistreated her at one time or another. Her aversion to men, Reid believed, was based in fear.

And that just wasn't right.

"Pig meat, Jinx." Reid waved the ham in the air, feeling about as idiotic as a man could get. "Bacon is tastier, I know, but ham is still a damn fine meat. This here is honey-baked, too. Good, right? If you come to me, it's all yours."

Other than a few anxious, needy twitches, the dog didn't

budge. Just alternated her gaze between his face and the ham, her dark, oval-shaped eyes filled with suspicion.

"Not happening tonight, huh?" Standing, Reid broke the ham into chunks and put them into Jinx's food bowl. He'd hoped the snack would be enough of a lure to draw her to him, but they'd been at it for a good fifteen minutes. Tormenting the dog into compliance was not on his agenda. "There you go, girl. Eat up. We'll try something new tomorrow."

He washed and dried his hands, leaned against the counter and removed the small envelope he'd stuck into his shirt pocket. Two messages for Daisy—one written, one sentimental—were tucked inside. He just had to figure out a good place to put the envelope.

A location she would come across naturally, but the girls would not.

The coffee canister, maybe. Or her purse, if he could get to it without Daisy seeing. Neither idea struck Reid as particularly original, though, and he sort of liked the notion of wooing her with a bit of creativity. He'd come up with something better.

Replacing the envelope into his pocket, he turned to leave, hoping to find Daisy in the living room. Earlier, he'd spoken to Erin and Megan about the likelihood of his moving out soon. It was time—or near time—that doing so made sense. For Daisy and the girls, so they could continue to grow closer without his presence acting as a buffer.

For him, too. As he and Daisy danced around one another—because he was far from giving up on her, on them—he thought a little distance would prove helpful. Hell, maybe he'd get real lucky and Daisy would actually miss him some if he weren't here every night.

At any rate, he figured enough fireworks were in their immediate future that having separate base camps would become a necessity. But he wanted to give her a heads-up and get her take on the option before he formed a final decision.

Jinx was now near her food bowl, licking her chops, apparently having finished her snack. His movement, slight as it was, caused her entire body to tense into stillness, and once again, he was met with a pair of dark and wary eyes.

Dog and man studied one another. Reid took a step forward. Jinx pivoted, so she had more space to maneuver, and retreated a few doggy steps. But she didn't growl. And she didn't seem all that interested in attacking his ankles.

Well. Perhaps he'd give this friendship thing another shot before seeking out Daisy. Sitting down, so he was somewhat closer to the dog's level, he said, "No more treats for the night, but how about a belly rub? Or maybe a scratch behind the ears?"

Tilting her head to the side, as if curious about where this conversation might lead, Jinx plopped her butt on the floor. So…they were back to sitting and staring, were they?

"You know," Reid said, "I don't believe you're really afraid of *me,* just my gender. At some juncture in your life, someone did something to you that made you fear men."

Little by little, Jinx's paws slipped forward on the tile, until her belly rested flat against the floor. She settled her long, narrow head on her legs and emitted a soft, keening sort of whine.

As if in agreement.

"Yup, that's what I thought. A man mistreated you, huh?" Reid frowned as he considered the many despicable methods a human being could use to inflict damage on an animal. "I gotta tell you, Jinx. That idea ticks me off. Makes me wish I knew that man's name and location."

Her left ear twitched and cocked in his direction, again forcing the thought that she wanted to make damn sure she caught every word of what he had to say. Nonsense, of course, but dogs were smart. Wouldn't surprise him in the least if she recognized his sincerity.

"But look, despite what this coward did to you, not all men are bad."

Offering a scratchy, gravel-coated grumble as a response, Jinx—without lifting her head from her legs—stomach-scooched forward a few inches. *Toward* Reid.

This seemed positive, so Reid continued to talk, keeping his tone in an easy, relaxed range. "If you give my gender a chance, I think you'll find that most of us are pretty good guys."

Another odd-sounding canine whimper emerged. In disagreement, most likely.

Or he could be losing his marbles. It was one thing to talk to a dog. It was another to believe the dog was an active participant in the conversation.

"I know. Difficult to believe when you've been burned once, but I wouldn't lie to you." And darn if the dog didn't ease herself forward another couple of inches. "I get being gun-shy, though. It's a natural state of being after someone has hurt you. And…ah…I respect your need for caution and vigilance, Jinx. I really do. You're just protecting yourself."

A visible shiver rippled along the dog's back. She kept her attention, her focus, solidly on Reid, and after a drawn-out huff, she edged herself toward him a little more. Now the distance between his knee and her nose spanned about six inches.

And Reid, sensing he was *this close* to crossing a barrier, held himself motionless. The last thing he wanted was to startle Jinx enough that she took off.

"Here's the problem, though," he said. "Remaining vigilant is smart only to a certain degree. There's a point where too much vigilance can stop us from experiencing a lot of good things. And—frankly speaking here, Jinx—missing out on the good isn't any fun. I guarantee—"

Elongated verbal sounds, rising and lowering in octave, erupted from the dog's throat as Jinx seemingly told Reid an impassioned story. He listened and nodded, as if he understood her, every now and then uttering, "Hmm" or "Is that so?" or "Really?"

This went on for two, maybe three, minutes, before she abruptly stopped and inhaled a long whoosh of air, and looked at Reid as if to say, "Well, now what?"

"Up to you, pooch," Reid said. "Whatever happens next is your call."

Without any further hesitation, Jinx pushed across the floor, erasing the remaining distance that separated them. Heaving a loud, breathy sigh, she dropped her head on his lap and bumped her snout into his hand.

"Friends, huh? Good choice," he murmured, stroking the dog's back. Emotion—entirely too sappy for a grown man's peace of mind—dampened his eyes, thickened his voice. "Thank you for the trust, girl. That took a lot of courage. I guarantee I won't let you down."

Jinx huffed a short and contented sound that, yet again, seemed to state she understood every word Reid said. And hell, maybe she did. Who was he to decree such a thing as impossible? He scratched behind her ears and under her collar, and it was then that an idea occurred to him. The perfect, creative place to put Daisy's envelope.

A place, he believed, she'd be sure to find both of his messages posthaste.

## Chapter Eight

Close to an hour after Daisy had retreated to the sofa, Jinx stumbled into the living room. Reid wasn't with her, so Daisy assumed he was still in the kitchen or had gone to bed. She hoped for the latter. The dog, in a plea for attention, whined in a long and plaintive manner before resting her paws on the edge of the sofa.

"What's wrong, sweets?" Jinx exhaled what sounded an awful lot like a heavy sigh of remorse. "Oh, I see. You gave in, didn't you? Feeling guilty for the price of that ham, hmm?"

Another whine, even more protracted than the last, coupled with an unflinching, dark-eyed stare. If Daisy didn't know better, she'd swear that Jinx was asking for forgiveness.

"Well, look. There aren't many females who can resist Reid Foster's charm," Daisy said, petting the top of Jinx's head. "And this seems a lot like the morning-after regrets. My advice? Don't beat yourself up. You enjoyed the ham, so you got something out of it."

She kept patting and scratching Jinx's short-haired coat as she spoke, not feeling strange about holding a one-sided conversation. A huge portion of her reasoning in adopting Jinx was for the simple comfort of having company.

Besides which, Daisy wasn't entirely certain that their conversations were one-sided. Whippets were extraordinarily intelligent, empathetic dogs.

"So," she said, "are you feeling a little better now?"

And, as if proving the accuracy of Daisy's thoughts, the dog vehemently shook her head.

"Trust me, Jinx. You need to let it go. But I'll tell you this—" Daisy fingered the dog's collar, which she'd just noticed was askew and looser than normal. "Oh. You're not upset about surrendering, are you? Good for you. Stand behind your choices."

Unbuckling the leather band, Daisy started to tug it in a notch when her eyes fell on a small, gift-size envelope that someone—Reid, of course—had strung through one of the collar's holes using a garbage-bag twist tie. Lovely. He'd had ulterior motives for kissing up to Jinx.

Daisy freed the card and tightened Jinx's collar to the proper fit. "There you go, sweets. Should feel much better now."

Jinx wagged her head once more, as if ascertaining the issue had been corrected, and—apparently satisfied that was the case—loped toward the stairs. Lately, she'd been sleeping half the night with the girls before rejoining Daisy on the couch.

Alone again, Daisy stared at the still-closed envelope in a mix of abject curiosity and outright denial. Today wasn't her birthday or a holiday. So whatever existed inside the envelope would likely fall into the range of another save-the-date card or an appointment-reminder card or...well, something equally as frustrating. She *should* toss the sealed envelope into the trash.

She should *not* give Reid the satisfaction of opening the

damn thing. Of reacting to whatever he might have stuck inside. That would be the smart, the…independent move.

She didn't do anything other than stare and wonder and…obsess a little. Giving in to her curiosity—sort of— Daisy gripped the envelope at the top right corner and brought it up to the beam of light coming from the floor lamp. And saw nothing.

No. She would not allow Reid or this stupid, nondescript envelope to bait her into taking one solitary footstep in his direction. Satiating her curiosity wasn't worth the consequences. Her resolve strengthened, Daisy swung her legs over the side of the couch and stood.

In her rush to get rid of the temptation, she half tripped, half skidded along the smooth hardwood floor, dropping the envelope in the process. And it made a flat, hollow sort of a *ping* that a lightweight card encased in paper should not have made, even against a rock-solid surface.

Kneeling, she used the tip of her finger to press against the envelope, this time feeling the definite impression of a small, circular object wedged in the bottom crease. Oh, no.

He didn't. He couldn't have.

But she knew that was exactly what he had done. In a flash, her willpower evaporated and she crumpled the rest of the way to the floor. Once again, her heart thumped in that too-fast, too-hard beat, and a strong shudder of melancholy forced her knees tight to her chest.

*Her ring.* That freaking envelope held her engagement ring.

Of course she opened it. How could she do anything other than rip off the side of the envelope and pour the ring into her palm?

A riptide of emotion engulfed her and she shuddered again. Swallowing, she looked at the tapered platinum band, the sparkling square-cut diamond and the twist of the birthstone-embedded love knot—garnet for Daisy, opal for Reid—that elegantly framed the solitaire.

He'd had this ring specifically designed for her, for them. To celebrate their love, he'd said. Their unique connection and the joining of their hearts, their lives.

Now, as they had then, tears filled Daisy's eyes.

Damn him for this, for putting such a visceral reminder of how much she'd loved him in her hands. One blink and a fat tear, and then another, rolled down her cheek. A silent testimony to the girl she'd once been, the love she'd believed they'd shared, the precious beauty of the moment she'd accepted Reid's proposal and he'd slid this very ring on her finger.

She'd never forget that night. Ever. They'd returned to Steamboat Springs after her graduation, after a celebration with their families, and he'd been quieter than normal. Contemplative. Rather than immediately taking her home, they'd driven for a while, just talking and laughing and…well, being them, she guessed. The couple they were at that time.

And he'd stopped his car in front of *her* house. Not her actual home, not where she'd grown up, but the charming, gingerbread-style house she'd adored since she was a child.

Daisy smiled now, in memory. When she was young, she'd pretend that fairies lived in the box-shaped, country-blue-and-white-painted house, with its profusion of decorative, intricately cut details edging the windows and the doors, the steep roof and the narrow front porch. She'd believed that house was magic, and she yearned to live there. With the fairies.

And it was there that Reid proposed. He'd promised that someday, they'd live in her magical fairy house. Would raise their children there, would love and laugh and create a life—*their* life—in the gingerbread house she'd always adored. And as they grew older and grayer, would sit on its narrow front porch in rocking chairs and hold hands.

Still in love. Still together.

Nostalgia, her past dreams and desires, whooshed in and emptied Daisy's lungs with a sobbing gasp. She'd said yes. Instantly and without reservation. Oh, she'd been so in love.

And in less than a year of that beautiful, miraculous night, she'd…left.

"Daisy." Reid's voice came from behind, low and evocative. Compelling and sensual. "Do me a favor and read the card before you throw the ring in my face."

Grateful that Reid could not see her cry, Daisy reached for the card. The glossy red front contained no words, no pictures, no clue at what she might find written within. The sick, slick glaze of fear coated the inside of her stomach and clogged her throat. Yes, she was afraid.

Almost desperately so.

Not *of* Reid, but *due to* his insistence at achieving that which she did not wish to surrender. How stupid, to believe she could keep him at a distance, her emotions—past and present—at bay. Now, by the single gesture of his giving her this ring, she recognized how delusional those beliefs were. How could she erect a strong enough shield to withstand this?

She wiped her cheeks with her arm, straightened her spine and cracked open the card. Familiar, bold handwriting filled the small space, and almost at the same instant she began reading, Reid recited his own words to her.

"Once upon a time, a boy loved a girl and promised her the world," he said. "The girl accepted and returned the promise, and they were to live happily ever after." Before she could inhale another breath, Reid's hands were on her shoulders. "Nothing has changed, Daisy. I still love you, and I still want to give you the world. All you have to do is say yes."

Sitting down, Reid cradled her body with his legs and wrapped his arms around her, gently pulling her backward until she rested against the firm wall of his chest. And being there, with his warmth and strength surrounding her, felt good. Right.

Imminently so.

The word *yes* danced on her tongue, and how...how crazy was that? Each one of her reasons for staying clear of this entanglement, of him, remained valid and powerful. He wasn't asking to date her or get to know her all over again. He was asking to *marry* her.

After an eight-year absence.

"I can't say yes," she whispered. "The idea is ludicrous."

"Is it, though?" he asked, his hand now resting above her heart. "In here, Daisy—where it counts—does the thought of becoming my wife and spending the rest of your life with me really feel so preposterous that it's beyond consideration?"

*No.* God help her, the thought of marrying Reid— even under these whacked-out circumstances—no longer seemed as outrageous, as unthinkable, as it should.

Admitting so would put her into a vulnerable and unsafe position. But she couldn't outright lie to him, either. So what she said was "My home isn't here, Reid. My life isn't here."

"That isn't an answer to the question I asked, darlin'," he said, rubbing his thumb along the side of her cheekbone. "What I think is that you can see us together as clearly as I can, but something is holding you back. What's holding you back, Daisy?"

Oh, Lord. He had to stop touching her. Had to stop talking to her in that warm, wholeheartedly intimate voice. Had to stop... He just had to stop. Because each second that passed weakened the thin line of her defense. It was as if each word, each caress, sent a jolt of electricity straight into her brain, shaking her thoughts, her arguments and her beliefs.

If this kept up, they would collapse into a pile of mush, and she would succumb. Allow his thoughts, arguments and beliefs to filter in, where they would grow in strength until she wouldn't be able to see past them to her own. She *knew* this to be true.

Out of nowhere, an image appeared in Daisy's brain. Of Erin sitting on her bed, clutching that pillow to her chest, adamantly refusing to play with Jinx, even though that was so obviously what she yearned for. From stubbornness or fear or something else?

Daisy still didn't know, but the image, the memory, struck a chord that resonated deep within. Was she doing the same? Maybe.

She looked at the engagement ring and had to stifle a sob. As glorious as her memories were, she could not find a way to believe that Reid would have proposed to her prior self if she hadn't formed her personality, likes and dislikes, around his.

And that truth right there negated every last word he'd said since her return. Any love he might profess to feel toward her—then and now—could not be trusted or believed in, based on her past inability to be her real self *with* him. She couldn't change what was already done, but she could—if she found the courage and strength—change the present.

*If* she found a way to remain wholly herself, to not fall into her old habits, maybe…maybe a second chance could exist with Reid.

"Daisy, baby, talk to me," Reid said, his mouth close to her ear. "Tell me what's churning in that head of yours, because this silence is killing me."

Tightening her hold on the ring, she balanced each of her thoughts and emotions and worries against the other, untangling the knotted mess they had become so she could view them separately. And she chose strength, courage and…knowledge.

Of their past, of what could be. She chose to try.

"You're right in that there are lingering feelings here, between us," she said, her voice quiet. Clear, though. This admittance, she knew, was as vital for her to say as it likely was for Reid to hear. "I'm not agreeing to a wedding, but I am willing to consider the possibility that…that we are not done. And I'm willing to put some attention toward that possibility."

"Attention toward that possibility, huh?" His voice, the gentle pressure of his arms and the firmness of his hold, didn't waver. The only sign that her words had impacted him in any way was his quick intake of breath. "Be clear here, Daisy. What do you mean by that?"

"I mean…" Hell. What *did* she mean? "No guarantees or anything, but I guess you could say I'm interested in spending time with you on a…a personal level."

"So we're dating? As in bowling and movies and candlelit dinners?"

"Um. Yes? But we can skip the bowling," she said, going for lighthearted. In truth, her heart hung so heavy, it could have been an anchor. What was she doing?

*Trying,* she reminded herself. She was *trying.*

"And…shall I take all of this as a maybe, then?" He didn't have to explain the origin of his question. Not when his engagement ring lay in the palm of her hand. "Or are we still locked in a definite no for the time being?"

"Not a definite no, but…" Oh, God. Did she really want to go as far as a maybe? She shook her head. "Not a maybe, either. Somewhere in between, I guess."

His jaw brushed her cheek. "Any answer above a no is a gift."

"I just…I don't…I can't…" *Breathe and calm down.* "No promises."

"Okay," he said without qualm. "No promises. Just… hope."

*Hope.* Suddenly, the moment became a little too overwhelming, so Daisy scooted forward a few inches, out of Reid's arms. Twisting to face him, she opened her hand to look at the ring. And her deep, deep yearning expanded. "I think this is the most beautiful ring any man has ever given to a woman, but I can't keep it. Not unless…that is—"

"That ring has always belonged to you," he said, his voice and gaze intent. Serious. "And if you give it back, I'll just keep finding inventive methods to repropose. Over and over and over." Now he spoke in a light, almost teasing manner. "Could be fun, I suppose."

"I can't keep this," she repeated. "I haven't said yes."

"You can, and I believe we've already established we're at the not-yet-a-maybe stage." He moved forward, decreasing the distance she'd put between them. "I'm not asking you to wear the ring, Daisy. I'm asking you to…safeguard it. That's all."

Before she could decide whether she should argue or agree, Reid pushed himself even closer. Heat flickered to life, pumping through her entire body with a rush of sensation and longing. His intent, she knew, was to kiss her. Fully, soundly. Just as she'd imagined earlier.

And, oh, she wanted that kiss. Wanted his mouth to capture hers and take control. Wanted nothing more, in fact, than to feel that familiar pull of his body to hers and hers to his, the power of their desire, in the joining of their lips. More than a want.

She *craved* his touch, his kiss.

As if he could read her thoughts, his hands came to her face to cup her cheeks. His deliciously dark eyes, sinful and beautiful and filled with all of the promises she wished she could believe in, met hers. He bent his head downward and her lips parted in anticipation.

Currents zapped in the air—electricity of their own making, of the unique heat they created together—and her body, as if on its own accord, leaned toward him. In eagerness and hunger and a desperate, almost frantic type of need that stole her breath.

That last bit was what unclogged her circuitry and kicked her rational brain to life.

"Stop," she whispered, pushing her empty hand against his shoulder. Their lips were, maybe, separated by the width of a solitary strand of hair. So close she could almost feel him, taste him. She pushed again, harder this time. "No kissing."

A kiss would lead to sex. And sex would lead to falling too fast, which would then cloud her ability to coherently assess her feelings. Simply speaking, sex muddled everything.

"No…kissing?" His gaze, still dark and heated but steady, locked on to hers.

"No. No kissing," she repeated, forcing strength and surety into her tone. She didn't know how successful she was since the pounding of her heart reverberated louder than the volume of her voice. Space. She required space. She slid backward. "No touching, either."

Reid's brow quirked. "Are we setting rules now?"

Well, she hadn't thought of it that way, but… "Yes, that's exactly what we're doing."

He tapped his fingers against his leg. "Of course," he said, his voice smooth and rich, "you rightly pointed out that you didn't have to accept *my* rules. But I should accept yours?"

Flustered, from the almost kiss and the exchange, Daisy nodded.

"Not sure that's entirely fair," he said easily, without so

much as a bat of a lash. "How about if we compromise? We each get to set…oh, let's say three rules. And we each agree to accept and follow both sets of rules from the start."

She gripped her fist tighter. On the surface, his suggestion came off as logical. But she didn't have the slightest doubt that there was a catch. Something he wanted from her, maybe. Or something he wanted her to do that he didn't think she'd go for.

Of course, she could do the same.

"I don't know," she said after a deliberately long pause. "What if you set a rule that I don't like or vice versa? We need veto power. One veto each, no questions asked."

"So I lay out my three rules, you do the same and we can each strike one from the playing field. Why, we'd only have two rules each, and I really had my heart set on three."

"No, no, no." She almost laughed. *Almost.* "You state your first rule. I either agree and accept or I veto. Then it's my turn to state my first rule. We go back and forth until we've each set our three. But," she said, "we each only get a single no, so we have to use it wisely."

"Seems you've thought of everything." Reid stroked his jaw, as if in contemplation. "Fair enough. But you know that good manners—meaning, ladies first—dictate that you should start."

"Happy to." Her goal was to get him to veto right off, before she instituted her no-touching-or-kissing rule. And there was no way he'd agree to this. "My first rule is that you move out of this house. Tomorrow, after we have a chance to talk with Erin and Megan."

"It's a solid swing if you're angling for a veto," he murmured, his tone even and his features composed, "but you're forgetting a few key facts. You and the girls are accustomed to each other now. And frankly, now that we're dating, I sort of like the idea of picking you up and dropping you off. More traditional that way." He winked. "More romantic, too."

"So you're saying…?"

"I agree to your first rule."

"Are you quite sure?" she asked, shocked by his agreement. "What if this upsets the girls? I thought you were all about not changing anything else in their worlds right now. And Erin still isn't completely comfortable with me, so I'm not sure—"

"I already agreed, Daisy." Reid made a tsk-tsk noise. "But to calm your worries, the girls are fine with the idea of my moving out. We talked about it earlier, when we were outside with the snowmen." At her questioning look, he said, "It's time. And I'll still be around every day."

Ah. Well, then. And he was right, she supposed, but that didn't alter her surprise. Or the fact that she now had to come up with something else for him to veto.

"Okay," she said. "Your turn."

"*My* first rule is you have to help with the wedding planning, as if you have accepted my proposal." Before she could object or veto, he held up a hand. "Now, don't get all fretful. This won't equate to anything other than what I've said. There isn't a hidden agenda. I just want you to be a part of the planning."

"Wh-why?"

"Because, then, if your not-yet-a-maybe becomes the yes I hope it will, our wedding will actually be *our* wedding. Seems important, is all."

"I… That doesn't strike me as…" Aargh! Why couldn't she talk? Think? Or, for that matter, breathe? "What, exactly, do you envision this help entailing? Be specific, please."

"So businesslike." Quick humor darted across Reid's face. He reined it in and said, "You offer your heartfelt opinion, Daisy. On everything from the ceremony to the reception.

Select a wedding dress—I'll pay for it, of course—and...I don't know, whatever else a bride needs to get married. Basically, the whole shebang."

*Trouble.* Of the triple-shot-of-insane variety.

There were reasons—a gaggle of them—why this was so *not* in her best interests. Of greatest concern, though, was with how she'd reacted to the ring, to his sentimental card and the near-kiss. She feared—just by taking part in the preparations—that she'd become far too immersed in the situation, too attached to Reid's vision to see her own.

But damn it, if *this* was his first horse out of the gate, what were the other two? She couldn't chance losing her one and only veto on something so relatively straightforward.

"Fine," she said. "I accept rule one."

"That, my dear, is very good news."

Hmmph. He didn't appear disappointed. Rather, he had that satisfied, cat-with-a-bowl-of-cream glitter in his eyes. Possibly, she'd just made a mistake.

"Rule two," she said, thinking quickly, "is that...if my not-yet-a-maybe does not become a yes within a week of May sixth, you cancel the wedding. All of it, from beginning to end."

Probably, he'd nix this rule, and then she'd be able to institute her no-kissing-or-touching mandate. But if he didn't, she'd at least be secure in the knowledge that his muleheadedness wouldn't put him in an untenable, uncomfortable situation come May sixth.

She hated the thought of that scenario repeating itself.

"Veto," he said without preamble, causing her to inwardly wince. "That one's dead in the water. Come up with another."

"No kissing." Why, oh, why, was he so determined to see this wedding through? Shouldn't her agreement to date be enough for the moment? "Or touching of an intimate nature."

"What if you instigate the kissing or the touching?" he retorted. "May I then return the kiss or the touch, or…?"

"Yes, but I don't expect that to happen," she said with a hard swallow. Not for a while, anyway. "And it's your turn."

"Right." Rubbing his hands together, he said, "My second rule is that we will, at some juncture in the near future, have a no-holds-barred discussion about our past."

"That isn't a problem, Reid. I figured we—"

"There's more, Daisy," he said, his voice muted. "I will want to know every thought that led you to leaving that morning. And then—" he exhaled a constricted breath "—I want the opportunity to speak my piece."

Hmm. None of what he'd said seemed to be asking for too much, but goose bumps dotted Daisy's skin and pinpricks of alarm appeared. "Is that everything?"

"Yes, other than it's my call when we have this conversation."

"Okay. That's…fine."

"You accept?"

"Yes." Despite her unexplainable foreboding, she wouldn't deny either of them a conversation they needed to have. Besides which, she'd left him with a letter on their wedding day. This was the least of what she owed him.

"All righty, then," Reid said. "Your third rule is…?"

"No avoiding of the truth, fibbing or creating any attention-stealing diversions if I ask you a point-blank question," she replied. "You have to answer. Completely and honestly."

This, she hoped, would give her the ability to keep future surprises at a minimum.

"I'm committed to honesty, Daisy, and—"

"I'm not calling you a liar," she clarified. "I just don't want to show up for what I think is a lunch date, and find a roomful of people expecting us to get married. And don't tell me such a scheme is beyond you, because I know better."

He grinned. "See? You know me as well as I know you. But I'm fairly set on May sixth, so you have nothing to worry about in that regard."

"Right. Nothing to worry about," she muttered. From her perspective, she saw plenty to keep her awake with concerns. "Your turn. What's your third rule?"

"Pretty sure you'll veto this one."

"Try me."

"From now until May sixth," he said, his voice and demeanor very much that of a resigned man, "we talk for no less than thirty minutes each day. By phone or in person, I don't much care. But every day, I get thirty minutes of your time."

"That's it?" Narrowing her eyes, she sat up straighter. "Your final rule is to *talk* to me?"

"That's what I said, isn't it?" Leveraging his weight on the palm of his hands, he leaned backward and stretched his legs. "Not such a difficult request, I don't think. Though, I'll completely understand if you choose to pound your metaphorical gavel in outright rejection."

Why hadn't she prevented the freaking wedding-planning imperative? Leave it to Reid to start with his most significant rule instead of a red herring, accurately pegging her unwillingness to get rid of a veto too soon. This rule, on the other hand, meant nothing to him.

Unless…oh. Maybe he *had* saved his most significant rule for last, and he was using *this* rule as the red herring. Meaning, he had another rule, the one he really wanted to put through, one she would highly object to, waiting in the wings.

Not that it mattered. The request was simple and straightforward, so she had zero reason to kick it to the curb. "Good try, but I'm not biting."

"Biting? Not sure I'd object to *gentle* biting, but—"

"Drop the act, buddy," she said with a sniff. "I am not

saying no to this. You want to talk with me every single day between now and May sixth? Fine. I agree to the rule."

The satisfaction was back, all but oozing over his expression, making Daisy believe that *this* had been his goal all along. But why? What was so important about making sure she'd speak with him every damn day?

"Excellent," he said with his trademark wicked-grin-and-a-wink combination. "And just think, we might end up with a story worth telling our future grandchildren. Wouldn't that be something?"

"Yep. That would be something." Still irritated and confused by his last rule, she pulled herself to her feet. "Since we're done and I'm tired and this is the room where I sleep—until tomorrow, anyway—I'd appreciate some privacy."

He was off the floor and approaching her before she finished voicing her request. Despite her bout of irritation, she was captivated by the look of his long-and-lean, tough-and-rugged frame in motion. And with no warning whatsoever, her craving for him and his touch reignited

"Wh-what are you doing?" she stammered when he stopped in front of her. Far too close for any sense of self-preservation. "Do you…ah…need a definition of the word *privacy?* Because invading my personal space does not liken to—"

"Not trying to invade anything," he said, kneeling down by her feet. "But you dropped your ring. And while I could buy another, my greater preference is to not lose this one."

"That's… I didn't realize." She inhaled a lungful of air. "I'm sorry. I had no idea I'd—"

"Nothing to be sorry about. The ring is here, safe and sound." With that, he stood and pressed the ring into her palm. "Keep this, Daisy, whether you choose to wear it or not."

Again, she closed her fist around the ring. Again, she

shuddered in melancholy and loss. Right or wrong, she wanted to keep the ring. "If…if you're sure, I'll hold on to it. For now."

"I'm sure." Lifting his hand, he brought it as close to her cheek as he could without skin meeting skin. Her face warmed even without the physical touch. "May I kiss you, Daisy?"

*Yes.* "I don't… No. Not now. Not…yet."

"Okay," he said simply, his voice soft, his gaze securely holding hers. "I'm curious about something, though."

"What…um…might that be?"

"Why try to cancel this 'probable sham of a wedding' merely a week before May sixth? Why not outright cancel it altogether?" He paused, as if to let his words, his meaning, take root. And, oh, did they ever. "You could have, you know. After I vetoed, you had the control to stop all of this 'wedding nonsense,' and you chose not to. I find that…interesting."

The power of his statement rendered her speechless. She noiselessly shook her head back and forth as his words looped in an endless circle in her brain. Why hadn't she, indeed?

One more long, intense look—as if he were trying to peek into her mind—before Reid stepped away, giving her room to breathe. "Sweet dreams, Daisy."

Then he left her alone. With her thoughts. Her worries. Her confusion. Not the least of which was why she hadn't considered, even for a second, doing what he'd just suggested.

Because he was right. Absolutely correct in his assessment that she'd had the control, the ability to put an end to all of this wedding insanity tonight, the second she'd received his veto.

And she hadn't.

## Chapter Nine

The following morning, Reid surveyed Parker's bedroom. He'd made the bed with clean sheets, vacuumed and even wiped off the light film of dust that had accumulated on the maple dresser and the nightstands. All of his belongings were packed and ready to go, and so far as he could tell, he hadn't forgotten anything. The room was ready for its new occupant.

And, after talking with the girls over breakfast—which had proved challenging food-wise, since Megan had declared today the color pink day—he believed they were also ready. Or, he corrected, as ready as they could be. A few questions were asked, a few sad looks were given, but Erin and Megan understood that Reid was not vacating their lives. He'd still see them every day. If they needed him, he was a phone call and a short drive away.

Sighing, he grabbed his two bags and went downstairs. He wanted to stop by his house and unpack, settle in a bit and—if he could fit in a shopping trip—hit the grocery store before his shift on the mountain that afternoon.

He deposited his luggage by the front door and turned toward the living room. Despite his belief that moving out of the Lennox household was the right step to take, he felt

strangely lost and…deflated by the prospect. Waking up tomorrow morning without the chatter or exuberance of two
little girls as his alarm clock would seem empty.

And lonely as hell.

Before he could sink too far into his gloomy thoughts,
Jinx roared around the corner of the archway. Seeing Reid,
she slammed on the brakes and slid to a skidding halt, just
short of impact. She gurgled a yelp of surprise, but…that
was it. No growling. No ankle tugging.

"Hey, girl," Reid said, hoping the peace they'd found in
the kitchen hadn't evaporated. "Where were you headed
off to in such an almighty rush?"

Her tail swished along the floor. And while she watched
him with interest, there didn't seem to be the same level of
wariness in her gaze. Good signs.

"See?" Reid said, petting the dog. "I'm the same guy
today I was last night. Still your friend. Still won't let you
down. Promise." Jinx snorted one of her canine replies
and pushed her head upward, against Reid's hand. "You
like that, huh?"

"Oh, she isn't picky. Any sort of affection makes her
happy," Daisy said, walking into the entryway from the
living room. Stopping, she crossed her arms over the navy-
blue-and-gray sweatshirt she wore, eyeing Reid and Jinx
with curiosity. "How'd you pull this off, anyway?"

"Patience." Standing straight, he grinned. "Perhaps a
touch of that obstinate nature you continually accuse me of
having. We also," he said, nodding toward Jinx, "had quite
the conversation. She told me a story you wouldn't believe."

Daisy's lips quirked at the corners, and humor—as bright
as the sun—glimmered in her eyes, over her expression.
"Is that so? Which story did Jinx…ah…share with you?"

"If I told you, I'd be breaking a confidence. Sorry, can't
do that."

"Uh-huh." She waited a beat, then said, "Seriously, I

have a few male friends, and they've tried everything to get Jinx to like them. Nothing's worked. So what did you do?"

*Male* friends? As in actual, platonic friendships or… more? Jealousy, swift and fierce, heated Reid's blood. Not a condition he experienced often, but the thought—the mere suggestion—of Daisy being romantically or sexually involved with another man did not sit well.

And that, Reid recognized, was a massive understatement. In truth, he had the sudden urge to stand over Daisy with a sword, protecting her from any man who might get it in his head to so much as *think* about looking at her. Ridiculous. Overkill. Way too cavemanlike.

But damn, that was how he felt.

Wasn't as if he'd give in to such an urge. Besides which, hadn't she described herself as a single woman on the very night she'd returned to Steamboat Springs? Yup, she had.

Once his blood cooled a few degrees, he shrugged. "Not much of a secret. I kept trying, kept reminding Jinx that I wasn't someone she had to fear."

"That can't be all there is to it," Daisy said in obvious doubt. "This is a huge accomplishment. Even the rescue agency stopped trying to retrain her. She… They called her a difficult-to-place dog. She required a female-only household."

"We reached an agreement, I guess." Reid scratched behind Jinx's ears, considering their exchange and then how similar his give-and-take with Daisy had progressed. Both scenarios had included talking, promises and…quite a bit of floor-scooting. He almost laughed. Daisy and Jinx had a hell of a lot in common. "Boiled down to plain old patience and the Foster mulishness."

"Well…whatever or however, thank you."

"Welcome. I was on my way to say goodbye to you and the girls when Jinx demanded my attention," he said. "Where are Erin and Megan? I expected they'd be with you."

"Upstairs. Going through the snow-magic book again, ascertaining they didn't forget anything." Daisy glanced toward the stairway. "They thought we'd hear from Parker by now, that he was coming home today. I told them that even magic can take a while to work."

"Ah." Reid had worried about this, but shooting down two little girls' hopes with the cold truth of reality was not something he would do. "I'll go on up and talk with them, see if I can find a balance between their belief in magic and honest expectations."

"I… That would be good," Daisy said. "Also, did you have some type of a conversation with Erin and Megan about who would take care of them if Parker died?"

"The night you got here," Reid said, thinking back to that evening. "The girls had watched this movie about orphans, and Erin had some concerns. She wanted to know who would take care of them if their father died. I mentioned you as one of the possibilities. Why?"

He listened as Daisy explained what had happened during their drive to the hospital. Why hadn't he connected the dots between Erin's behavior toward her aunt and the conversation he'd had with her? All of this time, she'd been suffering, scared that her dad might never come home, and Reid hadn't known. It made him feel about two inches high.

No. Shorter.

"I'll talk to them about that, too," he said, glancing at his watch. "I should probably do that now, before too much more time goes to waste."

"Wait! You don't have to move out," Daisy said, speaking so fast that her words merged into and on top of one another, and a rosy blush spread across her nose, her cheeks. "I hadn't meant for that rule to go through. I thought you'd veto it, and…"

"I know." Unable to stop himself, he moved closer to Daisy. "And if I didn't believe the girls or you were ready, I would've said no. But you are, they are, and I... With what's going on with us, leaving now is logical. Besides which," he said with a wink, hoping to lighten the moment, "if I stay, I'll have difficulty abiding by your no-kiss, no-touch rule."

Fine eyebrows arched in amusement. Or annoyance. One of the two. "You break that rule and I'll break one of yours. Or an arm. Which of the four is most important to you?"

"Go for the arm. The rules are far more important," he said, captivated by her eyes, her lips, her hair...hell, all of her. "Do you realize how astonishingly beautiful you are to me?"

"Um...no?" The rosy blush traveled from her cheeks to her neck to the glimpse of her collarbone. She rolled her bottom lip into her mouth before blowing out a breath. And all he wanted to do was pull her into his arms. "I'm just me, Reid. Nothing special."

"And that's where you're wrong. You're entirely special."

Blinking rapidly, she dropped her vision away from his. Embarrassment or pleasure? He hoped for pleasure, but guessed a combination of both. "I...well...um..."

"When someone offers you a compliment, the proper response is 'thank you.'"

"It's just that I—" raising her chin, she once again met his gaze with hers "—don't know if you see me as I really am. I'd like to change that. I'd like to...be myself with you and...um... What I mean to say is—" She stopped, breathed. "Thank you, Reid."

"Welcome," he responded. Where had she been going with that? He started to ask when he noticed a loose eyelash on Daisy's cheek. "I'm about to touch you," he warned. "But not intimately, so there isn't any call for slapping or kicking or fussing of any kind."

"Okay?" she said with another blink.

Approval enough in his estimation. Gently, he lifted the lash from her skin and placed it in his palm. Showed it to her and said, "Make a wish, Daisy." She swallowed, nodded. And he blew the lash from his palm into the air. "There you go. Hope the wish comes true, darlin'."

Rubbing her cheeks, as if to erase the pink glow she must know was there, she said, "You continually surprise me, Reid Foster. Sometimes, I think I'm ready to kill you."

"And what about those other times?" Probably, he shouldn't tease her, but the impulse was too great to resist. "Your thoughts have anything to do with kissing?"

A tremble of a smile appeared. Not all the way there, but damn close. "Maybe." The slightest of shrugs. "Maybe not. That's for me to know and you to...wonder about."

Oh, he would. Without a friggin' doubt.

"We're still good to go?" Anxiety, sudden and dartlike, pierced his gut and dried out his tongue. "All that we discussed...those rules and dating. Giving us a real, solid shot. Nothing's...ah...changed there, correct? No new qualms in the light of the day?"

"Morning-after regrets, you mean?" For some unknown reason, she laughed. "I meant everything I said. So, yes, we're still good to go." Another swallow, this one heavier than the last. "But no guarantees. That part hasn't changed, either."

Well, that was good enough for him. When he considered where they'd stood this time yesterday, a far sight better than just "good enough."

"Haven't asked for a guarantee. Don't particularly want one at this moment, anyhow," he said, speaking from the heart. "I'm...pleased enough with our current level of progress."

"Pleased *enough?* What more could you want from me?"

"Now that's a question." Reid ran his hand over his jaw. "Where to start? With a kiss or deciding some of the details for the wedding or straight to the honeymoon?"

"Did you have an accident sometime over the past eight

years?" she asked, her voice modulated and serious. "Something that might have caused…oh, I don't know, a brain injury?"

"Nope." He knocked his fist against the side of his head. "Rock-solid. All of us Fosters are blessed with hard heads. In fact, you might hear from my family soon. My mother or my sister or…hell, any of them might call or stop by."

Just that fast, her complexion went from pink to alabaster. "Wh-why might your family call or stop by?"

"They're helping with the wedding details, of course."

"They *know?*"

"I wouldn't think of getting married without telling my family, Daisy. Now that would be insane," he said. "You remember how they are. Can you imagine—"

"Possibly," she said with a temperamental flip of her hair, "you might have considered planning what I *have* agreed to before a freaking ceremony I have *not* agreed to. I said I'd date you, Reid. Not marry you. I can't believe you told your family! They…they…"

"Had to tell them. They'd have found out anyhow." True enough. They would've. Every member of his family had the ability to scent out secrets with the accuracy of a bloodhound. That being said, he wisely chose not to share he'd *asked* for their help. "And I have set up our first…odd to call it our *first* date. Friday, all day. I'll pick you up in the morning, after the girls leave for school. Haley will be here when they get home."

"I haven't said yes. I've said no. I've said not-yet-a-maybe, but I haven't said yes," Daisy mumbled, more to herself than to Reid. "And he told his family. His *family.*"

"Ah, Daisy? Still here. No reason to refer to me in the third person." She worked her jaw, but not a solitary sound emerged, and she squeezed her hands into fists. *Uh-oh.* "Guessing you need a little alone time right about now," he said. "I'll…ah…go talk with the girls. Make sure they know I'll be around tomorrow afternoon. Maybe we can all visit Parker together."

Eyes as green as they could get bore into him, but she still didn't utter so much as a syllable. So that, along with the smoke he could almost see pouring from her ears, made him think that he should, possibly—and just until she calmed some—get the hell out of Dodge.

Being a man who listened to his instincts, Reid blew Daisy a kiss—since he couldn't give her a real one just yet—and took the stairs to the girls' bedroom. Two at a time.

Pink day had started out easily enough with a breakfast consisting of strawberries-and-cream oatmeal. Lunch—with overly milky tomato soup, the final slice of ham and a tube of fruit-punch-flavored yogurt—had been managed. Dinner, however, was proving problematic.

Megan did not want any repeats, and there just wasn't one other food in the house that remotely resembled the color pink. Daisy knew this, as she'd scoured the cupboards, the pantry, the refrigerator and the freezer a total of three times.

"We might have to pick a second color, peanut," Daisy said, using Reid's nickname for Megan. "For this meal only."

Setting her mouth into a stubborn line, Megan gave her head a firm and decisive shake. "It's pink day. Pink clothes and pink food and *everything* is supposed to be pink."

"I realize this," Daisy said calmly. "But unless you're okay with oatmeal or another bowl of tomato soup, we're clean out of pink food."

"No. Don't want oatmeal or soup."

Both of the girls had reacted in different ways to Reid's departure. Megan's mood had slipped into the grumpy range, while Erin had returned to her withdrawn persona.

Believe it or not, until now, Megan's crankiness had been easier to handle than Erin's distance.

A well-placed tickle, for example, brought forth a squeal of giggles in the younger Lennox daughter. Erin, however, seemed uninterested in any and every type of activity Daisy had attempted. Including playing with Jinx. This time, at least, Daisy understood the crux of the problem—Erin missed Reid—and believed she'd adjust to the change in schedule once she saw that Reid would, indeed, be stopping in every single day.

Focusing on her older niece, Daisy said, "Any pink food ideas, Erin?"

"Don't know." Erin ate a bite of her macaroni and cheese. "Pink lemonade and pink marshmallows?" She wrinkled her nose. "Oh. Daddy sometimes eats pink fish."

Salmon, probably. "Don't think we have any pink fish lying around," Daisy said. "We could go to the store. Do you like fish, Megan?"

"Fish sticks, but they're not pink." Rubbing her tummy, she frowned. "And I'm hungry now, so don't want to go to the store."

Tomorrow, Daisy promised herself, she'd go food shopping and buy a veritable rainbow of selections. "I know you're hungry, and I'm sorry, but we either put off dinner and go to the store or you let me make you something to eat that isn't pink." When Megan neglected to respond, Daisy said, "Or you can skip dinner altogether, and—"

Sighing in frustration, she crumpled her hair with her fingers. Nope, she couldn't go that far. Could not let her niece go without a meal. Somehow, she was going to have to figure this out. God. How did parents manage this sort of stuff on a day in, day out basis?

"It's a pink day!" Megan said again, planting her elbows on the table and her chin in her hands. "And when I had a blue day, Reid didn't make me eat foods that weren't blue!"

*Ouch.* Blue? Okay, then. If common sense wasn't going to work, Daisy needed to try a different route. She was good at creative solutions. Certainly, there was one to be found here. Sitting down in the chair next to Megan, she said, "Can you explain how you pick a color day? When you got up this morning, how did you know that today was a *pink* day?"

"Some days are any color days, like rainbows. Other days aren't." Megan pursed her lips into a pout. "I just know it. Inside. And today *felt* like pink, so that's what it is. Pink, pink, pink."

Not all that helpful. "What does pink feel like?"

Light brown eyes narrowed. "Like pink."

Oh, good grief. In another set of circumstances—such as watching a similar scene on a sitcom—Daisy would laugh. Not in this situation, though.

"Right. But what does pink feel like—" she tapped Megan's chest "—in here? Does it feel sad or funny or silly or mad? Does the feeling make you want to sing or…go outside and play?"

"It's…happy. Being happy," Megan said slowly, grasping on to Daisy's intent. "But not just happy. Warm and… and it's like when I'm on Daddy's lap and we're both covered in a blanket and we're watching TV or he's telling me a story or he's brushing my hair."

*Safe.* Pink meant safe for Megan. Nurturing, too, Daisy guessed.

Why pink instead of yellow or green or purple didn't really matter. Somehow, her niece had connected that specific color to how she felt when she was with her dad. And since the girls had awakened that morning thinking about their snow magic and their wish for Parker to come home soon, then of course today was a pink day.

Little-girl logic, perhaps, but Daisy totally understood. Now to connect that feeling of safety and parental nurturing to something other than the color pink. If she could. "Tell me something, Megan. When your daddy is home, what would he make for dinner if he wanted to make you laugh?"

"Pancakes," Megan *and* Erin said at the exact same moment. "With smiley faces!"

"Sometimes, he'll cook them in different shapes, too," Megan added, her tone heading from grouchy straight to exuberant. "Like hearts or flowers or stars. And we get to pick what goes in them! Chocolate chips or bananas or—"

"Apples and cinnamon," Erin interrupted, also sounding more upbeat. "And he always puts on this really funny hat and apron. And then he'll dance all around the kitchen and try to flip the pancakes high into the air. As high as the ceiling! And try to catch them again."

Megan blinked. "He's not so good at that. Once…once," she said, her laughter spilling into her words, "a pancake landed on top of his hat! And he said—"

"That he meant to do that!" Erin blurted. Then both girls were laughing so hard they had tears in their eyes and were almost doubled over in their chairs. A solid minute of hysteria passed before Erin caught her breath. "He looked so silly, Aunt Daisy!"

"I bet he did." Daisy could easily imagine her brother in the scene her nieces had just depicted. Grinning, she said, "He's a pretty great dad, huh?"

"He's the best dad ever! The bestest of the bestest!" With a sigh that must have reached her toes, Megan collapsed against her chair. "I don't like that he's gone, Aunt Daisy."

"Me, neither," Erin said. "I wish he was here now."

"I know, and I know he wishes he could be here right now, too." Small words to offer real comfort for such an intrinsic longing. Too small.

Megan's stomach rumbled. Loudly. "I'm still hungry, and now I miss Daddy a lot, and…and…" Trailing off, she crossed her arms over her chest, and with her defiant expression firmly in place, said, "It's pink day."

"Yep, it is pink day," Daisy agreed. "So we can go to the grocery store and buy some appropriately pink food. Or... we can skip a pink dinner and make pancakes together. And instead of waiting until after we eat, we can call your dad while we're cooking. If we put him on speakerphone, he can help us make the pancakes just like he does. Your choice, sweetheart."

"I...I choose—" Megan scrunched her face in concentration "—pancakes and Daddy on the phone! That will be as good as a pink day, I think. Better!"

Which was exactly Daisy's hope.

"What about me?" Pushing her fork into her barely touched macaroni and cheese, Erin frowned. "I already have my dinner, but I want—"

"What dinner?" Daisy hijacked Erin's bowl and hid it behind her back. She gave her niece an exaggerated wink and said, "I have absolutely no clue what you're talking about, Erin. I see nothing that looks like dinner around here."

More laughter ensued, and oh, was there a better sound in the world than happy children giggling? Daisy didn't think so. Nothing she'd heard had ever come close, anyway.

They dug out the hat—an extra-tall, fairly hideous in the comical sense, lime-green chef's hat dotted with bright red-and-purple hearts—and the oversize matching apron, which the girls insisted Daisy wear. So she did. Proudly, even.

And when they got Parker on the phone, he talked them through every step he used to make the perfect pancakes. If he told Daisy to dance, she danced. If he told her to flip the pancakes high into the air, she did...and even caught them more times than not.

Not a one landed on her hat, though. That was fine. More than fine, really. Some memories, some moments, shouldn't be touched. And that particular remembrance belonged only to Erin and Megan and Parker. She'd prefer to let it stay that way. Intact and…precious.

After dinner, the rest of the evening progressed in a much smoother fashion. Even so, there was another absence that couldn't be ignored. An absence that went by the name of Reid Foster. Naturally, the girls missed him. Unless there was another reason for her near-constant searching of the house and occasional whimpers, Jinx also missed him.

Without thought, Daisy reached for the long, sterling-silver necklace she wore under her sweatshirt, running her fingers along the chain until they closed around her engagement ring. She couldn't wear the ring on her hand, but she couldn't *not* wear it at all, either.

So, yes, despite her hope to the contrary, Daisy missed Reid, too.

## *Chapter Ten*

The first part of the week zipped by in a haze of activity. Sure, Daisy had already learned the basic ropes of her nieces' daily lives, but handling these myriad details without Reid's guiding presence—specifically, the morning routine—was almost an entirely new concept.

Something as simple as a misplaced shoe or forgotten lunch boxes or even the up-and-down moods of two little girls could throw an otherwise well-planned schedule into chaos. Evenings were easier, by a large margin. Reid would show up either just before or after dinner, and he'd jump in to help with homework, dinner or the girls' bedtime routines.

Strangely, perhaps, he didn't stay long once Erin and Megan were in bed. And, other than reminding Daisy about their all-day date on Friday, he didn't behave as if he were a man in love. He didn't try to kiss her or touch her or, hell, even converse with her beyond generalities.

A relief in some ways. Incredibly frustrating in others.

Probably, he was giving her space to come to terms with the agreement they'd reached on Saturday. Well, that or he was saving his energy for Friday, for whatever those plans entailed.

Regardless, by Wednesday morning, Daisy had decided to stop stressing over Reid's behavior and, instead, focus on what she could control. Starting with the practical, she wanted to clean the kitchen, deal with the laundry and respond to a few of the email inquiries she'd received from possible new clients. All of which were referrals from past clients.

But then, she wanted to visit with her brother.

While she had taken Erin and Megan to see their father the prior two afternoons, she'd yet to have any one-on-one time with Parker. His next—and hopefully, last—surgery was scheduled soon, this one meant to finish repairing the damage done to his leg. It was time, she believed, to have a conversation about their relationship, their family. A few apologies on her end, and a promise to be better, more involved, in the future.

And she didn't want to wait. Surgery was surgery. Anything could happen.

So, with this in mind, she hurried through her tasks and was almost ready to leave for the hospital when the chime of the doorbell rang. Not Reid, she guessed, as he typically let himself in. One of the neighbors, perhaps, wanting an update on Parker's health.

When she opened the door, however, the person waiting on the small front porch was not a neighbor. Rather, her visitor was none other than Reid's mother.

Margaret Foster looked much the same as Daisy remembered, with her straight, just-above-the-shoulders reddish-brown hair, warm sage-green eyes and smooth, lightly freckled complexion. Her petite and curvaceous frame carried a few extra pounds, and by sight only, she might be considered a soft woman. Daisy knew better.

Not only was Margaret physically strong from years of carting around trays loaded with dishes, but she was also, from the inside out, built of solid steel. She didn't mince words, she didn't disappear when trouble loomed and she'd go to battle for anything that mattered to her.

Especially her children. You didn't mess with the Foster kids unless you wanted to deal with their mama. And… well, Daisy *had* messed with a Foster kid. The firstborn, even. And she hadn't seen Margaret since the night before she was supposed to become her daughter-in-law.

Apprehension and, she wasn't ashamed to admit, fear solidified in her stomach. Even so, she metaphorically straightened her spine, and said, "Hi, Margaret. I… It's good to see you."

"Hello, Daisy," Margaret said with a small smile that didn't quite reach her eyes. "You don't look as if you were expecting me. Did Reid forget to tell you I was coming over?"

"He…mentioned some of his family might call or stop by, but—" She pulled in a breath. Oh, was he in trouble when she saw him next. "He didn't say exactly when."

The slightest touch of humor glinted in the other woman's gaze and teased into her smile. "Well, knowing Reid, I'm sure it was an oversight on his part."

Doubtful. More likely, this was his way of making damn sure Daisy was at home and not hiding out at the library or the coffee shop when his mother arrived. Because, yeah, that was probably what she would've done. What she said, though, was "Yes. Probably an oversight."

"I hope this isn't a bad time for you?" Margaret's voice, while not unkind, held the crispness of an under-ripe apple. "There are some basic details for the wedding that need to be settled before any other arrangements can be made. Won't take long, I don't think."

"No, no. Please come in. This is fine." What else was she supposed to say? Stepping to the side, so Margaret could enter, Daisy wondered what information Reid had shared with his family. "Did Reid tell you that I'm not... I haven't... That is—"

"That you haven't agreed to marry him? Oh, yes," Margaret said as she entered the house. "But he's also made it clear that we should proceed with the preparations." She regarded Daisy with a fair amount of curiosity. "I take it you're willing to help, despite your refusal?"

"In a manner of speaking, yes." Willing? Not so much. But if she expected Reid to abide by her rules, then she'd follow his. "Let's go into the kitchen and I'll explain. Over coffee?"

Margaret nodded. Then, seeing Jinx, who had finally poked her head around Daisy's legs, she said, "Why, hello there. Aren't you beautiful?" Kneeling, she held out her hand, and Jinx, always happy to make a new friend—of the female variety, anyway—rushed forward for love.

Several minutes later, once Margaret and Jinx had become properly acquainted, Daisy poured two mugs of coffee and brought them to the kitchen table.

"I'm not trying to muddle this...odd situation," she said, sitting across from Margaret. "But Reid is stubborn. He refuses to back down on this wedding idea, and I can't say yes. I—" she exhaled a breath, tried to steady her nerves "—*won't* say yes."

Wrapping her hands around her coffee mug, Margaret let out a soft sigh. "Ever?"

"I don't know." Daisy shook her head. "How can I know that? We... I've agreed to see where this—he and I—might lead. But I don't anticipate I'll have that answer by May sixth."

"And yet you're willing to assist in the wedding plans?"

"I don't really have a choice." She then attempted to explain the reasons why. The rules and how they came into being, his and hers. What she did not do was share the more intimate aspects of her feelings, her concerns…her fears. Those were private.

When she finished, Margaret chuckled. "He's a smart one, isn't he?"

"Too smart at times." Words, a million of them, crowded into Daisy's brain. Words she wanted to say. Words that Margaret deserved to hear. "I'm sorry for leaving the way I did," she said, allowing those words to spill from her mouth, her heart. "For whatever turmoil I caused. For hurting Reid. I was in a lot of pain that morning, and the truth is—" Daisy blinked to push away the sudden pressure of tears "—I just…I couldn't stay."

"Leaving him with only a letter was cowardly," Margaret said, speaking in a slow and steady beat. Still not unkind. Just matter-of-fact. "And yes, you caused him pain. He was devastated, nearly crippled by the loss of you. Ending your relationship in that manner wasn't honorable, Daisy. To you or to him, to all you'd built together."

"I'm aware of this now. Very much so, and I—" blinking harder, Daisy dipped her chin "—I wish I'd had the courage to do what was right then. I wish I'd somehow found the strength."

"Do you have the courage now?" Margaret asked, without even the slightest hesitation in her voice. "To do what is right, for both of you?"

"Yes," Daisy said, also with zero hesitation. "If similar circumstances presented themselves today, I wouldn't just run. I'd talk to Reid, face-to-face."

"And you won't accept my son's proposal unless you're absolute in that decision?"

"Correct. You have my promise on that, Margaret."

Silence, heavy with emotion, pressed in around them. Suddenly, Margaret reached over and grasped one of Daisy's hands. "I'm sorry, too, for what you had to go through that morning. Your parents made an unfair and thoughtless decision in the timing of that…confession. I had just as much anger for them, for what they did, as I had sadness for your choice."

This sentiment, and the truth behind them, shocked Daisy. Margaret was showing her grace and love when she could be—had the right to be—condemning and spiteful.

For a split second, she thought of her own mother, of the random attempts she'd made over the years to find some type of peace with her daughter. And how Daisy had not shown Clara Lennox the same grace that Margaret had bestowed on her. A troubling realization.

Shaking off the thought, Daisy said, "I mourned the loss, too. Of Reid. Of you and Paul, all of the Fosters. I couldn't wait to become an actual part of the Foster clan."

"We felt the same." Margaret squeezed Daisy's hand. "We loved you, too. All of us. And that, I think, made it more difficult to accept your choice. Or to easily forgive, because you were already a part of our family, yet you had hurt Reid so terribly."

"I understand," Daisy whispered, feeling every one of the regrets she'd claimed not to have. "I…would definitely handle that moment differently today."

"Well, then I think it's time for a fresh beginning." Margaret released her hold on Daisy's hand, and in the process, accidentally knocked over one of the coffee cups. The contents spilled onto the table and soaked Daisy's sleeve. "Oh! I'm so sorry. Are you okay?"

"I'm fine. Really." Fortunately, she'd dressed in layers that morning, so she unbuttoned and removed the wet shirt, displaying the powder-blue T-shirt she wore underneath. She grabbed a dishtowel from the counter, wiped the mess off the table and said, "The coffee wasn't hot anymore, so no harm done. Promise."

"I… Well, that's something, isn't it?" Margaret asked,

staring in the general direction of Daisy's chest. "You're wearing your engagement ring, Daisy. May I ask why?"

Crap. Just…crap. "Reid insisted I keep the ring, for safeguarding." Tightening her fingers around the ring, Daisy searched for an explanation. "I didn't want to lose it, so…"

"Ah. Well, yes, that makes perfect sense." Margaret smiled, seemingly composed, but Daisy recognized the knowing gleam in her eyes. The same exact gleam she'd seen in Reid's eyes. Like mother, like son, apparently.

"I'd hoped to get to the hospital this morning," Daisy said quickly, in order to change the topic. "We should probably talk about these wedding details now. If that's okay with you?"

"Of course." Reaching into her purse, Margaret retrieved a small, wire-bound notebook. She opened it to the first page, displaying a neatly numbered list. "We need to decide the venues for the ceremony and reception. We can't do much else until we know the locations."

"Right." Daisy swallowed past the lump that had materialized in her throat and tucked the ring inside her shirt. Out of view. "I'm open to suggestions, so whatever you think is fine."

"It's what you think that matters here," Margaret said. "However, Haley and I did come up with several ideas, and I checked with the chapel you were to be married at before. They have room for a one-o'clock or a six-o'clock ceremony, but I wasn't sure how you'd feel about—"

"Not there," Daisy interrupted, her heart all but pounding straight through her T-shirt. She couldn't—wouldn't—allow Reid to stand at the same altar in the same church on the same date and…have the same outcome. "Actually, let's not repeat any of what was planned before. And I want to keep everything as low-cost, as simple, as possible."

Margaret's entire form stilled. She closed her eyes for a millisecond, as if in silent prayer. Upon opening them, she said, "Those are all conscientious considerations, but it occurs to me that if you were to change your mind, this will be your wedding day. Let's not go so far in the other direction that we lose any of the beauty that such a special moment should provide."

Oh, dear Lord. Somehow, Daisy now had two Fosters believing there would be—or, at least, *should* be—an actual wedding on May sixth.

"Please understand that this wedding is not—"

"Never say never, Daisy." The other woman's tone was once again crisp, but in decisiveness rather than coolness or uncertainty. "You don't know how you'll feel tomorrow, let alone by May sixth. Not with any clarity or certainty."

And there it was, Reid's bulletproof logic. Obviously, he came by it naturally.

"I suppose you're right," she agreed, mostly because arguing against the truth seemed illogical. She *didn't* know how she'd feel tomorrow, the next day or by May sixth. "But I still don't want anything planned that is too costly or extravagant."

"Agreed. Now," she said, crossing off several items on her list, "this might sound odd, but what about using Foster's Pub and Grill for both events? That will satisfy your low-cost requirement but allow me to—" she winked in a very Reid-like manner "—decorate with a wedding in mind. We'll be in our shoulder season, so can easily close to the public for the day."

Foster's Pub, from what Daisy remembered, had a somewhat old-world style of elegance and charm that shouldn't be overly difficult or expensive to transform for a simple wedding. More important, the place was familiar and safe, so when—if?—she did not change her mind, when—again, if?—she did not show up to marry Reid, he would basically be at home.

Surrounded by the people who loved him.

Which was probably the best, if not the only, way she could offer some form of protection, comfort, for whatever fallout he might experience.

"It's…a great idea." Perfect, really. "Let's do that."

"Wonderful!" Margaret said, beaming. "Morning or afternoon for the ceremony?"

"Um…I don't know." Overwhelmed, already picturing how the pub might look all decked out for a wedding, Daisy rubbed her arms to chase off her sudden chill of foreboding. "Seriously, I don't think it matters much. Whatever you decide is fine."

"I believe this is supposed to be your call." A brief pause. "So, morning or afternoon?"

Daisy focused on the wall calendar and recalled that May sixth fell on a Tuesday, then considered the practical logistics that any of Reid's guests would have to face. Giving in, she said, "Late afternoon. Four o'clock, with dinner after. But simple, all the way through."

Margaret nodded in approval and jotted down a note. From there, they discussed the reception in depth. Everything from food to entertainment to what freaking song should be played for Reid and Daisy's first dance as husband and wife.

As each decision was made, each detail set, Daisy forgot about the rule that mandated her input. She stopped thinking of the wedding as nonsense or as insane. She, instead, began to envision the wedding she'd truly want to have. *Her* wedding.

Not just that, but her wedding *to* Reid.

Almost without conscious thought, she took the rather large step from the not-yet-a-maybe stage into the maybe… just-maybe phase of possibilities. And for once, the overriding emotion that Daisy felt was not fear. It was hope.

Daisy sat across from Reid at the Beanery, Steamboat Springs' favorite coffee joint, in a billowy, scoop-neck bluish-green blouse and with a quirky, almost mischievous, grin on her face. She appeared pleased with herself, happier than he'd expected, and remarkably, not annoyed with him at all.

For five full days, Reid had done his level best to give Daisy some distance, some peace and quiet, to consider all they'd discussed on Saturday. Her admission that she still had feelings for him had hit dead-center, and suddenly, the stakes had shot sky-high.

To the point he'd considered calling a halt to every last bit of this wedding mess he'd created in favor of simply spending whatever time he could with her before she returned to California. In one instant, he'd wonder why he ever thought planning a wedding was a good idea, and in the next…well, he'd remember every reason he'd made the decision to begin with.

Ultimately, he chose to trust his initial instincts and keep the ball rolling.

And he'd done so by filling the first portion of today's date with a visit to the county clerk's office for a wedding license, which they couldn't actually file for another few weeks, but Reid had all he needed now in order to do that. Then they went to the florist, to select the flowers for their ceremony, and the bakery, to decide on a wedding cake. Both tasks were completed in shockingly short order. Daisy had known exactly what she wanted.

At the florist's, she'd asked for wildflowers in an array of vivid colors with something called silver brunia as a "unifying element," and at the bakery—without tasting any of the samples—she'd ordered white cake with lemon buttercream icing and raspberries.

Sounded good to Reid. But then, he wasn't all that choosy when it came to cake.

During their first nuptial go-round, he'd had one hell of an issue in getting her opinion on any of the wedding decisions. Mostly, he'd tossed out ideas until he'd seen a flicker of interest in her eyes or a smile of longing grace her lips. Indications he then used to narrow down the choices, until, eventually, their wedding and reception had taken shape.

That was fine then, and he'd deal with the same now if he had to. But he liked this change in Daisy. Liked that she felt comfortable, confident, to clearly and easily state her opinion. A sign she was becoming committed to him, this wedding, or one of maturity and self-assurance borne from the years they'd spent apart?

Could be both, he supposed. Would like to think that possibility held merit.

"So," Daisy asked, jumping clean into his thoughts, "what's next on the agenda? Your mother and I have the venues, reception menu and a few options for entertainment lined up. With the flowers and cake now taken care of, I'd say we're all but done."

"Oh, not quite yet," Reid said. Almost, though. Just a few more steps of the wedding-planning variety before they moved on to what he considered the real portion of their date. Well, the serious and hopefully romantic portion, anyhow. "Though, your willingness toward firming these details has come as a pleasant surprise," he said. "Are we to that maybe yet, darlin'?"

She tilted her chin, arched an eyebrow. "You asked—no, make that ordered—for my assistance. I'm good at getting things done quickly. Very good. And for this, I'd rather accomplish as much as we can, as fast as we can. Easier that way, since—" Here, she abruptly stopped and shrugged. "Just easier. Less stressful in the long run."

"Less stressful, how?"

Temper, just a flash of it, really, dipped into her expression. "I'm busy, Reid. With the girls and Parker, with arrangements for if...*when* I go home." She sipped her latte, her movements and body language tense. Quietly so, though, as if she were hanging on to her composure with every ounce of strength she had. "Uncluttering the nonessentials from the essentials reduces the stress. That's all I meant."

"Right. The nonessentials." Probably, he should be bothered by this claim, but her use of the word *if* in reference to returning to California held more weight, more importance, in Reid's mind. It also worked fairly well as a lead-in for some of what he'd hoped to talk about today. "What's it like, living in Los Angeles? Are you happy there, Daisy?"

"I'm…content. I enjoy my friends, my home. My job."

"Content is good," he agreed. "Content is, for most folks, more than enough, but I asked if you were *happy*. Do you wake each morning with the knowledge that you're where you're supposed to be, doing what you're supposed to be doing? Or are you…still searching?"

"Searching?" She gulped another sip of her latte. More as a delaying measure, he assumed, than from bona fide thirst. "What could I possibly be searching for?"

"Connections, maybe? You're all on your own out there, Daisy. Who has your back if you become ill or something in your life turns sour?"

"I'm not on my own. I have friends and…" When she looked at him again, the temper was alive and well, as evidenced by the bright green shade of her gorgeous eyes. Even so, Reid saw more than anger. He saw…loneliness. "What about you?" she blustered back. "Are you happy when you wake each morning, secure in your choices, your daily existence?"

"Depends on what aspects we're talking about. I love my work. Love living here, in Steamboat Springs, where my family and friends are."

"Which sounds awfully similar to what I originally said."

"Similar, yes. But, Daisy, unlike you, I absolutely have

regrets." He watched her closely, looking for a sign—*any* sign—that would state she'd missed him, longed for him, as he had her. "Decisions I wish I could do over, and—" Well, hell. There was Cole and Dylan entering the Beanery, a good thirty minutes ahead of schedule. "We'll have to finish this later."

Angling her head in the direction of Reid's gaze, she sucked in a breath. "Your brothers? Why am I surprised? I shouldn't be surprised." She returned her focus to Reid, and in a soft, tremulous voice, admitted some of what he needed to hear. "I wasn't entirely honest with you when you asked about… What I'm trying to say is that I am not without regret."

Damn it. He didn't want to wait until later, he wanted to hear this now. Sighing, he combed his fingers over his hair. A misstep, asking his brothers to join them. Hopefully one that wouldn't bite him in the ass before the day was over.

"Dylan and Cole are here to talk about the honeymoon," he said quickly, before his brothers reached the table. "And I meant for this to be fun and light. I'm sorry."

Just that fast, a mask of coolness slipped into being, replacing the conflicting emotions, the temper and the loneliness, that had been clearly evident. In a voice dripping with sarcasm, she said, "Oh, I can't wait. Our *honeymoon?* Really?"

"A mistake, Daisy." And damn it, after this he'd lined up what was sure to be another error. Well, he'd follow through and hope he could put them back on track before the day's end.

Now at the table, Dylan and Cole slid into the two remaining chairs. Dylan nodded in greeting and said, "Hey there, Daisy. Been a while, hasn't it?"

"Hey back, Dylan. And yes, it has." She flicked her gaze from one brother to the next. "Did you all phone each other this morning to discuss what to wear?"

It took a second for her meaning to hit, but when it did, Reid laughed. All three of the Foster brothers were wearing flannel shirts and jeans. "We have similar tastes. And you two," he said, directing his attention toward his brothers, "are early. Anything wrong?"

"Nah. Couldn't be helped, though," Cole said. "Mom and Dad need Dylan at the pub sooner than expected, so we thought we'd take a chance you'd already be here." He grinned at Daisy and waggled his eyebrows. "Nice to see you, Daisy."

"Nice to see you, too," she said, her tone friendly. Welcoming. "And congratulations! I hear you're getting married soon." She smiled in a sweet-as-saccharine sort of way. "I take it that you, unlike your brother, have a bride who has accepted your proposal?"

Dylan tipped his head back and laughed. Loudly.

"Yup." Cole's smile widened. "Rachel has, fortunately, agreed to become my wife."

"Well, that's really terrific. I'm happy for you," she said with a telling glance toward Reid. "And honestly? I *love* the concept of not planning a wedding until a proposal is properly given *and* accepted. Your brother could use some tips in that department."

"Sure," Reid said, not taken aback in the slightest. After all, the truth was the truth. "Maybe Rachel could give you some instructions in…oh, showing up for the wedding? Because I'd bet my last dollar that she'll be there, on time, ready to live up to her agreement."

"Whoa, guys. Chill." This came from Dylan. "Maybe Cole and I should take off?"

That, Reid thought, was a damn good idea. "Sorry for dragging you—"

"Oh, no. You asked them here. They get to stay." Daisy leaned the top half of her body across the table. Reid followed suit, so they were almost nose to nose. "Drop this now, Reid, before you spend another penny or waste anyone else's time."

"Not going to do that," he said. "So you might as well quit asking."

They stared at each for a solid thirty seconds before she withdrew and returned to her side of the table. "Stubborn fool of a man," she muttered, mostly under her breath. Then she held out a hand toward Dylan. "Might as well give me that file folder you're holding, so we can choose a honeymoon that will likely go to waste."

"Likely?" Dylan and Cole and Reid all said at once.

She blinked. Twice. "Just give me the damn folder."

Dylan, not having much choice in the matter, slid the folder to Daisy. She flipped it open, read through his list and looked over the various travel brochures tucked inside, seemingly uninterested in every last one of them. But Reid noticed that she stared at one for just a second longer than the others, and a glimmer of excitement, of yearning, appeared in her eyes.

Ah. He should've known. A tour, including overnight stays, in castles across Ireland. The magic and history of that experience would appeal much more to a woman like Daisy than a week-long ocean cruise or a hot and sandy beach in Hawaii or the Bahamas.

"Nope," she said, closing the file folder with a snap. "None of this is… I'm not choosing any of these destinations." She pushed the folder back toward Dylan. "A few days of camping and hiking will suffice well enough for this honeymoon, so…um…that's my decision."

Camping and hiking, eh? Sure, they could do that…in Ireland, in between castle hops.

"Sounds like a plan," Reid said, making a mental note to fill in Cole and Dylan on his true intent later, since they were handling the details. Hell. Maybe he could convince Daisy to go on a vacation with him, if not a honeymoon.

"Camping it is, then. Starry nights and sleeping bags and toasting marshmallows over a fire. Love the idea, darlin'."

"Of course you do." She rubbed her hands over her face and sighed. "One more item checked off the list. I'm almost afraid to ask what's next."

"Why, you should be able to figure that one out," Reid said with a wink. "There is one essential item that every bride needs, and that would be a—"

## Chapter Eleven

Wedding gown! The dratted man expected her to try on wedding gowns. Worse, she'd have to buy one, otherwise he'd probably yank any old thing from the rack and have it delivered to her door with some sweet, sentimental little card that would make her all gooey-eyed and emotional and then she'd have a physical reminder of May sixth taking up space in her closet.

Daisy closed her eyes and pushed out a breath. In all of her considerations about what this date—this all-day, freaking date—might consist of, she had not, even once, arrived at the conclusion that they'd be spending a chunk of their time in this fashion. She should have, especially after the visit from Margaret Foster, but she hadn't.

Still, a rule was a rule, so she'd rallied. Initially, she'd sped through every decision put in front of her, trusting her gut and that annoyingly clear vision of *her* wedding to lead her through the maze. That had worked well enough, and she'd held it together. For the most part, anyway.

Until she'd had to choose a honeymoon destination.

Honeymoons signified love and romance. Fun, laughter, maybe some frivolity. And sex. A lot of hot, lusty sex between the newly married couple. And for whatever reason, being presented with a host of brochures of potential destinations had brought her to her senses, reminded her of the honeymoon she and Reid had originally planned. All of their hopes and dreams for the future swarmed in next, and that had been enough of that.

She refused to select a location for a honeymoon that she just did not believe could happen at this point in time. But if she did believe, if all of this was *real,* she knew exactly where they would go, exactly which destination she would've chosen. Ireland.

Since it wasn't and she couldn't, she thought of where they were—the Rockies—and went with camping and hiking. Cheap. Easy to cancel. No fuss, no muss. And, yes, she'd been quite pleased with herself for solving that not-so-little dilemma without breaking down or ripping those damn brochures into shreds.

Or reaching across the table to strangle Reid.

But now, while he was off doing God knows what, she was stuck in a bridal boutique with his sister, Haley, and Cole's fiancée, Rachel Merriday.

He'd literally walked her inside the boutique, ascertained that Haley remembered she was watching Erin and Megan after school, reintroduced her to Rachel—whom she'd met a few times when they were younger—and said he'd return in an hour or two. And then he'd left.

*An hour or two.* Awesome. Somehow, Daisy promised herself, she'd solve this ridiculous dilemma in far less time than that. She just hadn't yet figured out how.

"Stop looking so glum," Haley said, her attitude just as upbeat and bubbly as Daisy recalled. She'd always liked Haley. Still did, and under less weird circumstances, would've wholly enjoyed the reunion. "I know this isn't the most ideal of situations, but try to have fun…and, I don't know, let's look for a dress that isn't necessarily only meant for a wedding?"

Rachel, who reminded Daisy of a runway model, spun around in a circle with her arms spread wide. "Sure," she drawled, "because there are so many nonbridal gowns here to choose from."

"Maybe with alterations or…I don't know." Haley chewed on her bottom lip as she surveyed the shop. "We'll find something."

"Why are you two doing this?" Daisy asked, unable to keep the question to herself any longer. She'd stayed mute on this topic with Margaret, and again with Cole and Dylan, but now…well, now she wanted to know. "Why support Reid's insanity?"

"Because he loves you," Haley replied instantly and with full sincerity. "And I love him, and he asked. Reid never asks for anything from any of us. Plus…well, you could say that I understand where he's coming from. I…um, sort of followed a similar path not that long ago."

Rachel half snorted, half snickered. "Your path was far more convoluted," she said, still laughing as she scanned through a rack of gowns. "You followed Gavin home, went against most of what he told you, coerced him into a weekend alone and…hmm. I guess that about covers it."

Twirling a chunk of hair around her finger, Haley grinned, apparently not offended in the least. "And look where we are now. My methods were unusual but successful."

This, Daisy knew, was a story she'd like to hear. Not now, though.

"As for me," Rachel said to Daisy, "I've learned that the Fosters do not go to such extremes unless they are very certain of their feelings. And as long as I've known Reid, I've never seen him behave like this, which tells me he's serious. So that's why I'm helping."

"Rachel also has a better understanding of your side of the equation." Haley pulled out a long, frothy concoction of a wedding gown and went to a mirror, where she held it in front of her body. Shaking her head in rejection, she said, "Tell her, Rach."

"Let's just say that Cole wasn't entirely sane in his methods of pursuing me, either. And—" a light blush stole over Rachel's cheeks "—I sort of turned the tables once I discovered what he was up to, so I'm not exactly blameless in the playing-games department."

*Okay, then.* "I have no idea how to respond to...to any of this," Daisy admitted, feeling more overwhelmed than ever. "Other than I'm beginning to believe that every one of you is—"

"Crazy? Impulsive?" Haley offered with a light grin. "Don't worry, we're aware."

"I don't know," Rachel added. "I'd just go with...happy."

*Happy.* Reid's earlier question revived itself in Daisy's mind. Was she generally happy with her life in California? She'd thought she was. Had believed so until...well, until recently.

"What about this, Daisy?" Haley asked, holding up another voluminous, frothy gown. "Doesn't this look like something a Disney princess would wear?"

"It's pretty, but...not my style." The gown was beautiful, but had far too many beads and pearls for Daisy's taste. If she wore that gown, she'd feel as if she were the wedding cake. Of course, that shouldn't matter. Not unless she actually decided to be a bride on May sixth. "On second thought, that will work just as well as anything else. I'll take it."

"Um. No, you won't," Haley said. "Finding the perfect wedding gown is a process. I think Rachel tried on close to... Oh. Wow. Daisy, look at the dress Rachel found."

She was already looking. Already captivated.

The V-neck, crepe-backed gown that Rachel held was sleeveless with a light, delicately embroidered lace overlay that extended from the narrow straps at the shoulders all the way to the floor-length hem. If there was a train at all, it was short, perhaps two or three inches lower than the front of the gown. And there was not one bit of froth, not one inch of the ostentatious, not one pearl or bead or sparkly sequin to be seen.

Just simple and lovely and romantic and, yes, perfect.

She knew better, but she tried on the dress, anyway, and once she had, she couldn't leave the boutique without purchasing the gown, without allowing the bridal attendant to take her measurements for alterations. As fate would have it, the dress was almost a perfect fit, and would be ready for Daisy to pick up in a matter of weeks.

Which seemed to prove that this simple and lovely and romantic wedding dress was *supposed* to be hers, and, after very little deliberation, Daisy decided to trust those instincts.

Perhaps she was just as crazy as Reid, after all.

Yup, he'd definitely misfired.

When Reid returned to the bridal boutique to collect Daisy, Haley had already left to pick up the girls from school. Rachel and the love of his life were sitting on one of the benches outside the shop, and were involved in what appeared to be a somewhat deep conversation. Upon seeing him, both had clamped their mouths shut, looked at each other and, as if on cue, started talking about a host of rather inane, unimportant topics.

The weather. That white was the most popular car color. And something to do with Disney princesses and frothy concoctions that Reid couldn't make neither hide nor hair of.

So, after ascertaining that Daisy had, indeed, selected a wedding dress—though she refused to allow him to pay for it, and he'd yet to determine if that were a positive or a negative—he'd thanked and hugged his soon-to-be sister-in-law, and once they'd said their goodbyes, he focused on the remaining hours of his date with Daisy.

On the woman herself.

On the conversation they needed to have, and if that went well, perhaps some romance to round out the evening. Perhaps, if he were very fortunate, the kiss he'd been dying for since almost the moment Daisy had returned to Steamboat Springs.

And if none of what he planned went well, then what? Well, Reid wasn't quite sure on that front, but he figured he'd deal with that particular outcome if and when it presented itself.

Still, he'd misfired. He shouldn't have spent so much of their day on extraneous details that might or might not have any bearing. But what was done was done.

Now all he could do was step forward and hope for the best.

"Close your eyes, sweetheart," he said to Daisy, who was staring out the passenger-side window in utter silence. "I have another surprise, and this one has zilch to do with May sixth."

A small sigh emerged, but she faced front and did as he asked, and said, "In less than a day, we've planned the majority of a wedding, I've seen most of your family in one fell swoop, and seriously…I'm not sure I can take a lot more. I…might just want to head home soon."

"That's your call," he said, making a right-hand turn onto the street where he lived. "But if you can give me a few inches of additional rope here, my hope is you'll change your mind."

"A few inches? I've given you several feet of rope already."

She had. More rope than necessary to hang himself with, if he wasn't careful. Metaphorically speaking. "I agree.

And I appreciate your patience. Now, though," he said as he pulled his SUV into his house's driveway, "I want you to open your eyes."

With a soft whoosh of air, she did, and then…nothing. Her entire body stilled as if frozen, and several seconds later, a shivering type of shudder stole through her, shaking her shoulders, her arms, and when she lifted her hand to her mouth, her fingers trembled.

"This is my house. *Our* house," she said, her voice a mixture of confusion and emotion, desire and longing. "I…I don't understand why we're here, what you want from me, or… Why are we here, Reid? Is this… Are you trying to recreate the night you proposed? Or…?"

"This is where I live, Daisy," he said, his heart dancing a wild jig and his palms sweaty as all get-out. "I bought this place about three months before our wedding. Mom and Dad helped, and…well, it was to be a surprise. My wedding gift to you, to us."

"You *own* this house?"

"Yes. I have for just over eight years now." Unbuckling his seat belt, he twisted toward Daisy. "I told you when I proposed that this would be our home. The place where we would raise our children, and fate must have agreed, because the house went up for sale a few months later. As I said, my parents helped with the down payment, and I bought it. For us."

"But then I left, and…and…" Repeating his actions, she unlatched her seat belt and faced him. "You've lived here all this time?"

Clean forgetting about rule number two, Reid trailed his fingers along Daisy's arm. "How could I do anything but live here? This house represents everything I wanted with you, everything I wanted for us…and Lord, you loved this place. How could I get rid of it?"

Her aquamarine eyes grew shiny with moisture. "I'm so

sorry, Reid. So sorry for not trusting in you, in us, enough to come to you on that day. I was so…scared and alone and I couldn't see how I could marry anyone, even you, even the man I loved, when…when…"

"We can talk about this right now, right here in this car, if you want," he said, feeling every ounce of her pain as if it were his own, and wishing desperately that he could take the misery away. "Or we can go inside. Maybe have a glass of wine, make some dinner and ease into this conversation. Again, your call. Whatever you want."

One tear and then another dripped from her eyes and coated her cheeks, and it was all he could do not to wrap her in his arms and just hold her. For however long she'd let him. But he knew—or sensed, rather—that what Daisy needed the most was some space to…breathe, he reckoned. Find her balance and the strength he knew she had.

"I believe I would like to go inside and have that glass of wine, relax and…I don't know, Reid, just spend some time with you that doesn't revolve around anything other than us."

"Exactly what I was thinking," he said. "So what are we waiting for? Let's go inside."

Even that took longer than it should have. Every couple of steps from the SUV to the front porch, Daisy would stop and shield her eyes against the late afternoon sun and stare at the house, from the steep angle of the roof to the narrow porch, to the rocking chairs he'd bought that very afternoon and placed just so…as a silent reminder of what he'd once promised.

What he still promised, if she'd…listen and accept and, hopefully, forgive.

She waited silently while he unlocked and pushed open the door, and when he offered her his hand, she took it without objection, and he led her inside.

Over the years, he'd slowly updated and decorated the

place, trying to envision what Daisy might have chosen for furniture or paint color or… Hell, how had he convinced himself that he'd moved on and had built any sort of immunity in regards to her at all?

Nuts, that. 'Course, he also hadn't strolled around each and every day with her in the forefront of his thoughts, dictating everything he did and said. She'd been more like a… whisper in his head, his heart.

"That glass of wine or a tour first?" he asked, recognizing the jagged quality to his voice. He felt stirred up and shaken, unsure of the direction to take, of what made the most sense.

She tightened her hold on his hand, and a surge of confidence eased some of his rough edges. Thank God for that. "How about both, at the same time?"

So that was what they did. He poured them each a glass of wine, though he'd have preferred an icy cold beer, and room by room, he showed Daisy her fairy house.

Most of the rooms were painted in actual colors, rather than the basic off-white. In the living room, he'd gone with a shade called oceanside that was almost a perfect match to Daisy's eyes, and a medium, earthy brown for the trim. The kitchen was painted a clean, clear blue that reminded Reid of a cloudless summer sky, and the master bedroom held hues of dove-gray and a hazy sort of *almost* purple his mother identified as hyacinth.

To him, it just looked like plain old gray with a shot of color, but who knew?

The remainder of the house held varying shades of browns, greens and reds. His furnishings were on the simple but sturdy side of the equation—nothing flowery or frilly—and while he'd hung a few paintings and pictures on the walls, he'd gone easy there, not wanting to live in too cluttered or crowded of a space.

"You've done a really great job with this," Daisy said,

her voice as soft as her eyes. "I love how you've surrounded yourself with color, with brightness. And I...not that it matters, mind you, but I wouldn't change too much. Some more decorations, maybe. Flowers and plants."

"I'm glad you approve." Now they were back in the living room, standing on opposite ends, and damn, he wanted her closer. "Unfortunately, I haven't found one sign that any fairies ever lived here. Hope that doesn't disappoint you too much."

A small, sweet smile lifted the corners of her mouth. "Oh, they definitely lived here. They just took extra care when they left to ascertain no one could prove their existence."

"Maybe they did, at that. I...still think of this house as yours. Ours," Reid said, speaking from the heart. Plenty enough time to delve into the rest. Later. "I'm pleased you're here, Daisy."

In the smallest fraction of a second, the ease and relaxation they'd been building faded into nothingness. A zap of invisible electricity whipped through the air, changing the energy, the tempo, between them into something different. Something acute and complex.

And, unless Reid was way off base, something dangerous.

"Pleased? How can you be so sure, so confident, that you're *pleased* when I'm—" she bit her lips together and unshed tears once again filled her eyes "—scared. I'm *scared,* Reid."

Her pronouncement must have shocked her as much—if not more—than it shocked him. She slapped her hand over her mouth and took two steps backward. Her eyes became more watery, and his gut twisted and tied itself into knots. She was scared...of him? Of them?

Due to her physical retreat, he forced himself to stand still even though every instinct he had begged him to go to her. Begged him to offer her his comfort, his strength. But he knew, despite her current emotional state, that Daisy was a damn strong woman.

She didn't need his strength. She needed his...understanding.

So, for once, Reid ignored his instincts and stayed put. "Honey, what's going on here?" he asked, keeping his voice even-keeled and calm. "What are you afraid of?"

"There are a lot of things I'm afraid of." Wiping her cheeks, her eyes, she inhaled a shaky breath. "Helicopters being one. Mice. I'd rather face off with a ravenous bear than a tiny mouse. Because I can see a bear coming from a long ways off. Oh, I'm not that fond of overly loud thunderstorms, either. Or skydiving. I tried that once, didn't like it at all." She shuddered, swiped at her cheeks again. "But what I fear the most is..."

Her words faded away. He waited, to see if she'd find the strength he knew she had. The strength to tell him what had her so upset, so...fearful. A million possibilities came to mind, and frankly, he despised every last one of them. Anything that could fill her with fear, he hated.

Simple as that.

She leveled her shoulders, lifted her chin, and he saw strength and determination and fierceness had replaced her tears. And that was good. Just as he'd expected.

"What I fear most," she repeated, "is letting people down. In not being whatever person they need me to be. My brother. My nieces. Once upon a time, my father. And now that you and I are on this crazy, unpredictable journey, I'm petrified of letting *you* down."

"Impossible, Daisy." He started toward her but she held up a hand, so he stopped. "You can't disappoint me. All I want is for you to be...I don't know, you. Just you."

"Exactly," she whispered, turning away from him. "And therein lies the problem."

"I have no idea what that means." Frustrated now, along with concerned, Reid gave in to his instincts and went to her. He didn't touch her, though, didn't so much as reach a finger in her direction. He just wanted to be closer. Wanted *her* to feel his presence. "Trust me on this, if nothing else. I *know* who you are. I've always known you. How can you doubt that?"

"How can I *not* doubt that when for my entire life— even when you and I were together—I've pretended, put on a show…an act of who I am, what I like and don't like, and become someone else?" Her tears poured heavily, in a flood of self-recrimination and fear. "You didn't fall in love with the real me, Reid. You fell in love with a woman who didn't exist."

"Untrue," he said, his voice flat but definitive. "I don't know who put that outlandish idea into your head, but I loved—still love—*you*. The woman standing in front of me now."

"You're wrong."

"I am not wrong." Difficult, but Reid managed to hold himself steady. Controlled. "Why don't you give me some examples of times you weren't you, in regards to our relationship—past or present, I don't much care—and we'll see if we can untangle this misunderstanding."

"Examples? Um." She blinked. "College. You said we should go to the University of Colorado, even though you were a year ahead of me, so we could be together. And I just agreed. Never offered another option. Because I didn't want to let you down or…or lose you."

"Now, see, I remember this situation differently." Reid backed off and leaned his weight against the sofa arm. "We each wrote a list of the colleges we were interested in, and the University of Colorado happened to be number one on both lists. It was the logical choice, but not the only choice. And you couldn't have lost me, even if you'd gone to school in Timbuktu."

"We did write lists, but…okay. Maybe I've recalled that moment incorrectly."

"I think you might have." He waited a second. "Any other examples you have spinning in that brain of yours you'd like to bring to the table?"

"What about Portelli's? How did that become our favorite restaurant? Or the details of our first wedding…the date, the chapel, all of it. I didn't offer any input, not because you didn't ask, but because I just went with whatever you said, and I didn't want to disappoint you."

If this matter didn't carry such weight, such importance to the core of who Daisy was, he'd almost have laughed. Lord, the woman was blind when it came to herself, to him, to them.

"Well, look. We went to Portelli's because I loved seeing you happy. We'd walk in, and you'd get this warm glow that had nothing to do with their food. You just liked the ambiance."

Her jaw dropped but she didn't say a word. Not one.

"As far as the details of the first wedding? Think back for me, will you?" While he could supply this answer just as easily as the others, he sort of wanted her to see the truth on her own. "How often did I flat-out tell you we were going to do anything?"

Dead silence enveloped the room while she pulled the past to the present. He didn't prod her in any direction, just waited. In patience and in love. In support and in understanding.

Now that it was brought to the surface, Reid knew exactly where this mentality had originated, but he'd never—not once—witnessed Daisy behave in the manner she described with anyone other than her father. Not with Reid, not with her brother, not with her friends. What she did do, what he'd always recognized, was her stalwart protection of her thoughts and that inner, secret world she hid from most everyone.

*That* was the Daisy he knew.

"You never told me we had to do or go or be anything," Daisy finally said. "What you did… Oh." Her shoulders slumped as the fight began to drain out of her. "You asked questions, tried to determine what I wanted, what I liked, and took those things into consideration as decisions were made. Is…is that right?"

"Close," Reid said. "Our entire relationship was always a compromise. I just had to work a little harder to ensure that happened, since you stayed inside your head so often. I'd like to point out that you do not do that anymore, Daisy. Not to the same extent."

"No…I guess I don't."

"Damn straight," he said, pleased. "Hell, you've had zero issues clearly and openly stating your opinion from the friggin' second I found you in Parker's living room."

"You're right," she said, her voice somewhat stronger. "I've fought hard to get to there, to be able to do that."

"You've succeeded."

"I have a question now." She moistened her lips. In nervousness, Reid guessed. "A point-blank, straightforward question, and due to the agreement of rule number three— my rule, that is—you have to answer honestly."

"And I will give you a wholly truthful response," he said, wondering where they were now headed. "My word, Daisy."

Expelling a breath, she nodded. "You say you know me, so tell me, Reid. Who am I?"

So many descriptions came to mind. Beautiful. Funny. Intelligent. Warm and loving and strong. But Reid did not believe those were the words she needed to hear. She wanted proof that when he claimed he knew her, he really did.

And while she might not appreciate or even get the comparison he was about to toss her way, he had promised absolute honesty. So that was what he was going to give her.

"I know you, Daisy. Very, very well. That isn't to say I know everything *about* you, because I don't, and I shouldn't. Exploration is a part of any relationship."

"That sounds a lot like surface talk, but what I—"

"Now, give me a darn minute here. I know what you want, and I'm about to tell you," he said, laughing. "If a... oh, let's go with a turtle and a porcupine. If those two animals produced offspring, then the result would be a creature who is...well, frankly, pretty much you."

Daisy's chin set in an irritated line. "You view me as a hard-shelled, prickly, nonexistent creature? Wow. That's quite the...association you've made there, and if that's what you think of me... I don't know why we're even having this conversation. *Is* that what you think?"

"Yes and no." Reid mentally formed the explanation that had made perfect sense to him less than a minute ago. "I believe you're a very strong woman, but inside, you're vulnerable. Fearful of sharing who you are with others. In order to protect yourself, you've built this facade of being fully independent, of not needing anyone else to...I don't know, exactly, make you happy or whole." He shrugged. "Something along those lines."

Her eyelashes fluttered and the tightness in her jaw lessened.

"And that facade is the turtle's shell, in case you're wondering." Hell. All of this had sounded reasonable in his own head. Verbally, though, he wasn't so sure. "When someone begins to move in past that shell, your vulnerability grows. So you do one of two things. You either become defensive and distance yourself as quickly and completely as you can—that's the porcupine comparison, because who wants to be too close to a porcupine?—or you go the other route—"

"And throw myself in so fully, that I begin to feel lost. Afraid."

"Which leads us right back to avoidance. Distance. Keeping yourself solidly in your own world, both physically and emotionally." Reid pushed himself off the sofa's arm and approached Daisy. "When someone hurts you, like your parents, you recede so far into your shell you… well, you're kind of hard to reach. I give you California as an example."

"I… Yes," Daisy said, her voice muted, her expression stricken.

"Here's what makes you amazing," Reid said, needing to get out the rest. "You'll sacrifice your protection for other people, for those who need more than they can do on their own. You bring them into your world, share your—" he grinned "—turtle shell and porcupine needles with them, and all the while, you're working on solving *their* problems."

"It's a nice idea, but—"

"Nope. I'm speaking the truth here, as rule number three dictates. Might take you a while to poke your head out of that shell long enough to see what's going on, but then… well, then there's no stopping you." He stopped, inhaled. "Look at how you responded to Parker's accident, and how you are with the girls? And hell, from what Parker has said, it's pretty much what you do for a living—solving problems."

She reached for support, found the chair to her left and gripped on tight. "I don't see myself as kindly, but I can't argue with the distance or the avoidance or the…fear and vulnerability."

"Look a little harder," he said. "Or just trust in me, in what I see."

"I don't... I can't... Okay, I'll try," she said, giving a short, jerky nod. "I've wondered, needed to know, if you really loved me. The real me. And if you didn't see me, that real version of me I've tried to hide, if you would be disappointed. If you'd still insist we should be together."

"Daisy, look at me." She didn't, just kept her vision firmly planted off to the side. "I see you fully, all of you. And I did love you. I still do, baby. And you've only disappointed me once, when you left. Just that once."

"Quite the huge disappointment, though."

"Won't argue with you there," he said, allowing a layer of his defenses to retreat. "And I have questions, some residual anger and confusion. I hope we'll work all that out, because I do believe—"

"You should hate me," she whispered, interrupting him, her voice too heavy, too dark for his liking. "After what I did, you should despise me. *That* would make sense. Why... why don't you hate me, Reid?"

"The reason is simple." Since touching her broke rule number two, he shifted so that he could see her face. So she could see his. "I'd rather love you. That's what makes sense to me."

"What am I supposed to do with that?"

"Oh, I don't know. Maybe—and this is just a thought, darlin'—maybe *let* me love you?"

## Chapter Twelve

Daisy couldn't breathe, literally, for a solid twenty seconds. All she could do, all she did do, was stand in statue stillness, and think of Reid's words, of everything he'd said.

Let him love her? Just...*let* him.

The thought was, at once, terrifying and electrifying, humbling and strengthening. But he knew her, he did, and that...well, that made the first step—*her* first step—a hell of a lot easier to take. Because that stubborn, stubborn man had been right all along.

She loved him. Had always loved him. Had never stopped loving him.

And, oh, Lord, the time they'd wasted, due to her worries and insecurities. Her lack of courage when she should have stood strong and believed, trusted, in their love. She didn't do that then, wasn't entirely sure she could do so now, but she could...*try*.

She looked at him, at this man she'd never been able to force from her heart, and he stood there, tall and straight and solid, so firm in his convictions.

He deserved the same from her. And so much more.

"Yes, Reid," she whispered, so afraid, so...*unsure,* of everything these words entailed. "I'll let you love me."

There wasn't a pause or a breath, just action. He came to her, pulled her into his arms and locked her tight against him. The softness of his flannel shirt rubbed against her cheek, the scent of him—rugged and clean and all man—surrounded her, and the strength, the blessed reality of his body pressed to hers, all served to calm her jumpy stomach and racing heart.

She'd yearned for, wished for, and had fantasized about this moment. And here it was…here *he* was, and she was so shocked, so damn grateful, she almost wondered if she were asleep in her bed and lost in one of her dreams.

"I have missed you so much, honey," Reid murmured, his voice soft and deep and sexy and sweet, all at once. "But I gotta ask about rule number two. May I kiss you now?"

A simple request, really, but a flash of heady warmth swept into Daisy's bloodstream, nearly buckling her knees with its potency. She looked up, and up some more, directly into Reid's eyes. They were dark and intense, searching and…well, beautiful. In so many ways.

She trailed her fingers along the angled edge of his jaw, felt the bristly roughness of his five-o'clock shadow against her fingertips and—standing on her tiptoes—brought her lips closer…closer…closer to his, and she kissed him. Fully. Soundly.

He groaned a needy, hungry sort of sound, and one hand came up to grip the back of her head, while his other lifted the hem of her shirt and found the small, tender area at the base of her spine. And the feel of his skin on hers dragged a moan from her throat, caused her temperature to rise another delicious degree. Or two or three.

Ever so slowly, Reid took control of the kiss she'd started, increasing the pressure of his mouth, his tongue teasing and tasting, savoring and exploring. And in no more than one combined beat of their hearts, pieces and parts of her soul she hadn't known were dormant shot to life. Along with this startling realization, the completeness she'd lacked for so long suddenly returned, filling her with absolute peace and now...now she understood what she hadn't before.

She could be, had been, *whole* without Reid, but she couldn't be, would never be, *complete* without Reid. The distinction between the two states of being was minuscule, perhaps, but profound. She belonged with him, he with her. Just as he'd said.

Also stunning was how her body recognized his, responded to his, instantly and without reservation. As they kissed, her nipples hardened and licks of desire, not so different from fire, swirled in her belly and between her legs, through and along and across every inch of her being.

She wanted him. Desperately and fully. In every way a woman could want a man.

Daisy was *this close* to unbuttoning, unzipping his jeans. *This close* to tugging the denim down, over his hips and off his legs. *This freaking close* to giving in to her hunger and her need and the bright, consuming energy that bounced and pulsated from her to him and back again, when Reid abruptly broke the kiss and stepped back.

Out of their embrace, away from...her.

The absence of him was immediate. Intense and heartbreaking. And, when she looked at Reid, he had a dark, haunted expression of...despair? Maybe. Maybe that.

Shudders of loss, of a different type of longing, replaced Daisy's desire. Confusion and uncertainty and fear rode in next, hard and heavy and unrelenting.

"Daisy," Reid said, his voice as ragged, as broken, as each breath he pulled in and pushed out of his lungs. "We need to talk. Before this goes any further, we need to have that honest, no-holds-barred conversation. Otherwise, we'll get too deep in for either of us to remain coherent."

Oh. *Of course.* "Your rule number two, I take it?"

"Yes. I wish we… Well, this has to be done. Simple as that."

Forcing her wobbly legs to move, she crossed the room and perched on the edge of the sofa. Her thoughts awhirl, her heart heavy, she delved in and spoke as quickly, as efficiently as she could, but with honesty. With all of her pain and remorse and sadness.

"I meant what I said earlier, about having regrets." A deep, cavernous sigh escaped as she considered her greatest mistake. "I should never have left in the way I did, and if fairies or snow magic could undo that choice, give me a second chance in that moment, I would handle that decision differently. Please believe that, Reid, if nothing else."

He sat on the chair across from her, leveraged his elbows on his knees and his jaw on his finger-laced hands. He seemed, she thought, tormented. And so, so far away from Daisy.

Impossibly far away.

"I do believe you, Daisy. I do." His brows drew together, his expression agonized and lost. Anger lived there, as well. She saw it, clear as day. "What I don't—can't—understand is how you were *able* to leave in such a manner, without an honest-to-God, real conversation. Hell, you didn't even call. How hard is it to pick up the friggin' phone?"

Strangely, as strong as her emotions were in that second, her eyes stayed dry. Her throat hurt from all she felt, though. And her chest had that hollow, frantic ache she remembered far too easily. Not as vivid or as sharp or as consuming, but there, nonetheless.

"Some of that has to do with what we've already talked about," she said. "After…after my mother told me the truth about my father, about her one-night stand, I tried so hard to believe in us, Reid. I did. But everything sort of collided in my head, and everything—even you and I—became this overwhelming mass of...confusion that I couldn't see beyond."

"One phone call, Daisy. One damn call and I would've been there, with you." Altering his position, Reid rubbed his hands over his eyes. "One call. That's all it would've taken."

A sob curled in the back of Daisy's throat as she listened, as she saw the damage she had done with her own eyes. "I just didn't know who I was, and I needed to figure that out, all by myself." Now, today, none of this sounded like enough of a reason to do what she had done, but it was the truth. Every last word. "So I could trust and believe in *me*. An identity that wasn't connected to my father or to you or to anyone else. And the reason I didn't call, couldn't call, was because I *knew* you'd talk me out of leaving."

He swore under his breath. "Would that have been so bad?"

"Then? I thought so. I believed the only choice was to start over."

"Without me?" Every muscle in his body tensed and grew hard. He snapped his fingers, saying, "Just bam, huh? Everything we'd planned, everything we were, you were able to throw it all out the window and run for the hills, *run away from me,* and start over. Wow, Daisy."

Oh, God. She found the chain around her neck, pulled it from beneath her shirt and held on to her ring—Reid's ring—as tightly as she could. For strength.

"Yes, I did that. In my confusion and shock over my mother's confession, nothing in my world seemed to make sense. And that included you. That included *us*." She tried to think, tried to find the exact right words, so he would understand. But she didn't know what else to say, other than, "I'm sorry. So sorry, Reid. I can't change this, and I can't go back in time."

Tension rippled and bobbed between them, around them, and all Daisy could do was wait and hope that somehow, in some way, Reid understood. That he would forgive her for her past mistakes, and remain true in his belief that they were meant for one another. A million years or merely thirty seconds might have elapsed, she didn't know.

Didn't care, either.

She was just grateful—eternally so—when he said, "Okay. I don't agree with that choice, will likely *never* agree, but I can and I do understand what you were going through, and how those emotions, that shock, scared you to the point you felt as if you had to leave."

"I would make a different decision today," she repeated. He needed to know this, believe this. "I *can't* promise I wouldn't leave, but I would talk to you. Let you know what was in my heart, and give you the opportunity to be a part of that decision."

"And that is enough. More than enough," he said. "I can let this go, Daisy. For us, for the future I hope we'll have, but there's something *I* have to tell you, and…" Yet again, despair and torment clouded his gaze. "This won't be easy, honey. And I'm sorry for that."

Warning bells screamed in her brain, and fear—cold and absolute—tarnished any relief she might have felt from his acceptance, from his willingness to forgive and move on. And she tried—Lord, did she try—to conceive of what he might have to say.

Of course, she couldn't. So she nodded and said, "I'm listening."

"Right. Here goes." A muscle tensed and then quivered in his jaw. "Not sure if you'll recall, but about a week before our wedding, we decided to take a day off and get away. We were going to hike, do some climbing at Rabbit Ears Peak, have a picnic and…just spend some time together, without the distractions of the wedding."

She nodded again. "I remember."

"You had some errands to run that morning, and something waylaid you—I don't know what now, can't put my mind on the specifics—but the point is, I arrived at your parents' house to pick you up before you'd returned. And…" He gave his head a hard shake, as if waking himself up or clearing his thoughts. "I let myself in, as I typically did."

Yes, Reid had been such a large part of the Lennox household, pretty much a member of the family, that he'd never had to announce his presence…not for years, anyway. That bit of what he said made sense, but her stomach twisted in apprehension.

She remembered that day. Remembered coming home and finding him in her room, sprawled out on her bed, with his eyes closed. And when he'd opened those eyes, they'd held the same look—the same freaking despair— she saw now.

"What happened?" she asked.

"Your parents were in the kitchen, arguing. They did not know I was there, based on the…volume of their voices. I… Well, I started to head their way." He paused, drew in a lungful of air. "I didn't know what I was going to do, exactly, but I thought they should know they weren't alone. I… Daisy, I didn't get that far. Wasn't able to do a damn thing before—"

"You knew," she said as her brain pieced together Reid's haunted look, what he'd already said and the time frame that this had occurred. "Oh, my God. You *knew*."

"Yes. Not all of it, not every damn detail, but enough to know that Charles Lennox was not your biological father, that you had no idea, that he thought it was time to tell you and that your mother refused. I heard her refuse, Daisy." Reid cursed again, somewhat louder than before. "And I hightailed it to your bedroom to figure out what in the hell I should do."

"You did nothing. That was your choice."

"Only for that moment." He was up and out of the chair,

approaching her before she could so much as blink. Sitting next to her, he wrapped his hand around hers. "It was the week before our wedding, baby. And I didn't want you hurt. I…wanted to protect you."

"Right," she said, trying to find some type of balance to get her through. "So you decided to do what my parents had done for my entire life and *lie* to me. How…how could you do that?"

"Not forever. No." His voice was firm and unyielding, as was the pressure of his hand, his grasp on her. "I was not going to lie to you. I was just going to wait, until after our wedding and our honeymoon, so we could keep that time of our lives whole and unsullied. And the thought of hurting you at all, ever, just about killed me. So, yes, I kept the secret."

"You shouldn't have," she said. "That was the wrong choice."

"I know," he said, his voice quiet and resigned. "And I'm sorry."

So many things could have been different if he'd come to her with what he'd learned. Discovering she was not Charles Lennox's biological daughter still would not have been easy. She still would have been shocked, upset, scared and confused. The truth of her parentage *still* would have shaken her world and everything she'd known, believed to be true.

None of those facts would have changed.

But if Reid—the man who loved her, the man who was to become her husband—had told her everything he'd heard, she would not have doubted in *them*. She *knew* this. Because what was marriage if not an alliance? Two people standing together, arm in arm, for better or for worse, in sickness and in health. Marriage was, in essence, a team sport.

And that right there, his presence during the worst moment of her life, would have changed *everything*. They would be married now. They would likely have children now. And they would be living in this very house, together, right now.

She wasn't so far gone that she couldn't turn the tables, couldn't see that if she had talked with him before she'd left, the same scenario could also be true. Daisy knew this, as well.

But she had years of reflection behind her. Years of believing that she knew everything there was to know about that morning. The specifics of what led to her mother's confession and Daisy's resulting beliefs, behavior and, yes, mistakes. This news, though, came at her with the force, the strength and the unpredictability of a tsunami.

Worse, this confession of Reid's brought back every damn emotion she'd experienced almost eight years ago. Again, her lungs refused to take in air. Again, she had the frantic need to get away, to leave, to go somewhere she could breathe. So she could figure this out.

Figure out, exactly, what to do with this information. Figure out how to erase the hollow ache that, once again, had taken over her entire being—body and soul—so she could regain the core of stability she'd worked so hard to attain.

Damn it! This was a lot, maybe too much, to absorb in this minute.

She tried to reel in her emotions. Tried to view this—the decision Reid had made—in a logical, rational manner. Reminded herself of all the valid reasons she should let this go. He'd let her transgression go, so she should do the same for him, for them.

But she didn't know if she could.

If marriage was a team sport, then love was...what? The warm-up stage? Maybe. Regardless, eight years ago, she and Reid—for different reasons—had absconded from the team…from *their* team. They hadn't turned to or trusted in the other enough to hold steady, to stand arm in arm against the world and do what was right.

And…no, she just couldn't let that go. At least, not enough to allow her to move forward with Reid or with the future she'd been so close to believing in.

Squeezing her eyes shut, Daisy searched for the words she knew must be said, for even the slightest strand of strength to yank on and pull close, so she had something to hang on to. "I understand your motivation in keeping this secret, so I can forgive that, Reid. I can, and I do. And while I know this is unfair, I can't…don't think I know how to—"

"No," he said, his hand tightening over hers. "Don't say what I think you're about to say. Just wait. Consider… remember that I love you, that I've always loved you, and that all you have to do is take a step toward me. Just one step, Daisy. That's it. I'll do the rest."

He made it sound so simple. So effortless. As if he were merely suggesting she take a physical step, rather than a metaphorical leap of faith. The problem, though, was that some leaps were far too treacherous, too steep and precarious, to trust in faith alone.

And in this case, she couldn't find the will, the courage *or* the belief to jump.

"I can't," she said. "I'm sorry, Reid, but I just can't."

## *Chapter Thirteen*

Spring had officially arrived in Steamboat Springs, date-wise, if not weather-wise, and the shoulder season had begun—meaning, the tourists had all but evacuated the city, and the residents were in relax-and-prepare-for-summer mode.

Reid hardly noticed the slowdown or the cool weather. In the twelve days following Daisy's rejection, he'd existed in an afraid-to-hope but afraid-not-to-hope state of mind. To counteract the negative side of the equation, he'd kept himself busy.

Today, as was the case most days, that included visiting Parker. He'd also been helping Cole and Rachel with their upcoming wedding. He was there for his family, personally and work-wise. And each day, he spent some time with Erin and Megan, as he wanted. As he'd promised. Those moments, though, were tough.

Not because of the girls, but because of Daisy. Even when she wasn't in the same room with them, he knew she was there, in the house somewhere, and while she wasn't exactly avoiding him, she had most definitely withdrawn into that tough-as-nails, prickly, turtle-porcupine shell of her own creation. And Reid did not know how to draw her out again.

Oh, he'd instituted rule number three—his rule, that was—and phoned her each night for their thirty minutes of conversation. But he did most of the talking. The first few nights, he'd tried to focus on them, on everything they'd already discussed, to no avail. Since then, he asked her questions. Almost any odd thing he could think of.

Parker and Erin and Megan, of course. Jinx. Daisy's life in California, her friends and her job. When they'd run out of air on those topics, he'd moved on to the sort of inane, unimportant subjects he'd heard Rachel and Daisy discussing at the wedding boutique.

And she answered every question posed, but only in the shortest method possible. She wasn't rude or unkind or even cold. Just abrupt and…well, sad. He thought she was sad. A thought that disturbed him to no end. *He'd* made her sad, and he wished to heaven and back that he knew how to change that status quo. To make her smile again.

Reid punched the appropriate floor level on the hospital elevator and waited while the doors swished shut, his mind still on Daisy.

Fortunately, he had some time left. A solid month before the wedding he hadn't canceled, the wedding he probably *should* cancel. Stupid to keep the thing going, especially because Reid didn't care if they were married on that particular day or not. Someday, whether on May sixth or ten years from now, he hoped Daisy would be his wife.

For now, he'd take whatever she'd give him.

But he'd gotten it into his skull that calling off the wedding would begin to shake his belief, his confidence in them, in all he saw for their future. So, no, despite his near certainty there would not be an actual wedding ceremony on May sixth, he could not, would not, turn away from the possibility. No matter how remote.

Daisy was here, in Steamboat Springs, and he figured she'd be here for a little while yet. Parker's surgery had gone well, but he'd still require a fair amount of support when he returned home. Reid did not have a shadow of a doubt that Daisy would stick around for the duration.

He had time, and that was the best thing he had going for him.

Clearing his thoughts, he stepped off the elevator and strode toward Parker's room, hoping to find his friend awake and in good spirits. Yesterday he'd seemed morose and out of sorts, clearly tired of being away from home, and ready to get back to his life.

Reid stopped in the doorway, looked in to make sure Parker wasn't asleep and grinned. Yup, today seemed better than yesterday. Not only was Parker smiling, but he also sat in a wheelchair near the room's large window. That was a good sign. Positive.

"I gotta say, this is a sight for sore eyes." Entering the room, Reid swung himself onto Parker's bed. "It's about damn time you got your lazy behind up and moving."

"Uh-huh. You're just jealous of all the attention I've received from the pretty nurses around here," Parker said, widening his smile. "But yeah, it's nice to be somewhat mobile."

"Understandable." Reid gave his friend a long look. "I've worried about you. Really am glad to see you're in a better frame of mind today."

"How can I not be? I am—" Parker mimed beating a drum "—going home soon. Possibly as soon as next week, depending on how quickly I can get up and maneuver without any help."

Now *that* was good news. "Well, then, I'd say your lazing-around days are over." Reid thought of the girls, of how excited they would be to hear that their snow magic, in a way, had worked. Their father was coming home ahead of schedule. "Do the girls know?"

"Yeah," Parker said, wheeling the chair closer to Reid. "They were here yesterday, and you should've seen them, Reid. With all their cheering and jumping, you'd have thought we were having a party that Santa Claus, the Easter Bunny and the Tooth Fairy were attending."

"They've missed you, so that's probably what it felt like," Reid said, imagining the scene. "Bet Daisy's pleased, as well?"

"She was. Is." An unidentifiable expression crossed Parker's face. "Though she wasn't thrilled when I mentioned our parents will be here soon. By the end of the month, or so. Once my father is given the green light for travel."

"Your parents are coming?" Reid inwardly winced. That would be difficult for Daisy. "Of course they are. I'm sure your mom's been a little nuts, not being here."

"Exactly." Parker gave Reid a long and steady look. "Works out well, in a way, since Daisy will be able to head for home once our folks have a chance to get settled."

"She's going home…at the end of the month?" Somehow, and Reid didn't know how, he managed to choke out the words. Daisy would be gone, back to her life in California, before May sixth. "I suppose that…ah…makes sense."

"No reason for her to stay, and my house isn't big enough to comfortably hold four adults, two kids and a dog. Besides," Parker said, "I've taken up enough of her time. I'm thankful she's stuck it out for this long."

"Right. Makes…ah…sense." Reid rubbed his temples. "End of the month, huh?"

"Yup, and you're repeating yourself now." Wheeling another few inches closer to the bed, Parker said, "You're also kind of green around the gills. Bother you, does it, that

Daisy's taking off somewhat soon? Anything you want to say about that?"

"Why would that bother me?" Reid said, not wanting to burden Parker with any of what he was thinking, feeling. "She has a life to get back to, and yeah, nice she's been here for you and the girls. Good for all of you, I'd expect."

"Has been, and I'm glad for that, too," Parker said. "I'd like to mention, just to put it out there, that other folks visit me. Neighbors. Friends. Your brothers have been by a time or two. Your parents stop in. Saw Haley earlier today, as a matter of fact."

Ah. Haley. That answered a few questions. "Well, my family is your family."

Parker reached for and grabbed an empty plastic water bottle, which he hurled at Reid's chest. Perfect aim. "You've been trying to convince my sister to marry you again, and we both know you've never gotten over her. What I want to know is…are you going to let her leave?"

"Only reason I haven't said anything on this front is I thought it should come from Daisy." Reid squeezed the water bottle, pretending it was a stress ball. "But to answer your question, I'm not sure I can stop her, nor would I want to. That's her call…."

"You love her, right?"

"I do love her." Reid tossed the water bottle back at Parker. He caught it with one hand.

"The woman I loved died, Reid. She's never coming back, and there's not one thing on this planet I can do to change that." Pain, fleeting but profound, deepened the blue in Parker's eyes. "You, on the other hand, still have an opportunity here."

"Do I? Doesn't seem that way." All at once, every damn doubt he'd tried to ignore surged forward. "Truth is, maybe I *should* give up. She took off, never once looked back, and I'm not blameless. I kept—"

"Well, not exactly. She did look back." Parker swore softly. "About a month after she left, she called you. I was there, answered the phone."

"Wait a minute. She called?"

"Yeah. You weren't doing well, and I was angry with my folks, angry at Daisy, worried about both of you. So I told her—" he cursed again, swiped his hand over his jaw "—to leave you alone. That she'd created enough havoc and that was the best she could do for you."

"Really wish you hadn't done that." He wasn't mad at Parker. Just stunned. This information sifted in with everything else, and rather than feeling pleased or relieved or…hell, hopeful, Reid was left with a sense of futility. "In a way, that's three strikes against us. Can almost make me believe that fate doesn't want us together."

"Three strikes? One is this, one is Daisy leaving, what's the third?"

"That I knew about her paternity and didn't tell her." Without mincing words, Reid related the facts of that situation. When he finished, he said, "Three decisions, three strikes."

Parker released a sigh. "If you hadn't so recently saved my life, I'd be honor-bound to kick your ass. You know that, right?"

"I know, and you still can," Reid said with a small, humorless smile. "Saving your life doesn't negate any of my mistakes."

"Why didn't you tell *me?*" Parker jerked his head to the side to stare out the window. There wasn't any true venom in his voice, just annoyance. "I love my mother and my father, but I hate that they did this to her. So yeah, wish you'd trusted in me."

"Couldn't," Reid said, speaking the simple truth. "If I was going to tell anyone, I would've told Daisy. She had to know before anyone else."

The men sat there in silence, considering what was versus what could've been. When Parker faced Reid again, his annoyance had vanished.

"Here's what I think," he said, his manner serious. "Perhaps you weren't supposed to marry Daisy eight years ago. Maybe these three strikes were meant to keep you apart *then,* for some unknown reason we can only speculate on. But then isn't now, and…if I had an opportunity to be with Bridget again, there isn't anything that would stand in my way."

Wise words, but Reid had already pushed against every barrier that Daisy had put in front of him. Now his instincts told him to step back some and give her room to breathe. He wanted Daisy to have the freedom to feel secure in the decision she'd already made, or—God willing—to come to a different decision and choose a new path.

One that included him.

So, he supposed he'd listen to another Lennox's wise words, and believe really, really, *really* hard that this time, Daisy would run toward him.

Standing in Parker's bedroom, Daisy stared at the lacy, romantic, simple wedding gown she'd picked up that afternoon—now altered to a perfect fit—and wished with every bone in her body she hadn't given in to temptation. She should not have bought this dress. What had she been thinking? Now this beautiful creation would go to waste, unworn and unneeded.

And that was just…sad.

Maybe, once she returned to California, she'd donate the dress. Maybe there was another woman out there who would take one look at this gown and declare it perfect. Already feeling the loss, Daisy carefully hung the dress in Parker's closet, where it would remain until she left for home. Another few weeks, maybe three. That's all she had to get through.

Parker would be home that very weekend, and her parents—God, her *parents*—would be here toward the end of the next week.

She pushed her palm against her queasy stomach in an attempt to vanquish her twisty nerves. Futile, she knew, while Reid remained in the house. He was downstairs with Erin and Megan, not to mention Jinx, right this very minute, and she'd…well, she'd chosen to hide.

Nothing had changed for her since that evening at her fairy house. She loved Reid. Now knew that she'd always loved him, and likely always would, but creating a life with him had gone from an almost yes—she'd been so freaking close—to a definite no.

Love did not necessarily equal a happily-ever-after ending.

Emotion, strong and overwhelming, came over Daisy in waves, but she did not cry. Could not cry. Sitting on the edge of the bed, she rubbed her temples and, for maybe the first time in her life, hoped for tears. Hoped for a temporary release of the empty, yawning ache deep inside that refused to dissipate. But, no. Nothing. Her tears, it seemed, had disappeared.

Or maybe, she'd simply used up her allotment. Maybe she'd feel this way for the rest of her life, with no respite, no peace. A horrifying thought.

Shaking her head to rid herself of that nonsense, Daisy pressed her hands against her eyes. Stood and headed for the stairs. She couldn't hide all night, and the girls needed dinner, and…as much as being around Reid hurt, she also yearned to stand in the same space with him.

Even if for only a minute.

Of course, later, she'd have his voice in her ear for *thirty* minutes. A shot of humor whisked in, dampening her anxiety and soothing her soul. Margaret Foster had been absolutely correct when she'd described her son as a smart man.

Due to that stupid, not-harmless-in-any-way rule, Daisy had to listen to Reid's voice—his ridiculously sexy, evocative voice—every evening. From now until May sixth. And, despite her sadness, despite the fact they talked about nothing of importance—he'd even stopped trying to convince her to change her mind—she craved these phone calls. Dreaded them, too.

It was in these moments, when there were no other distractions surrounding her, that she searched the hardest for the will, the courage, to take that jump. That freaking long and terrifying leap of faith, and every night as they said goodbye, she knew she couldn't.

So, yes. She craved the ability to talk with Reid, but at the exact same time, she dreaded the instant that, once again, she realized with crystal-clear clarity that nothing had changed.

On the morning of Cole and Rachel's wedding, Reid entered his brother's childhood bedroom in their family home to find Cole alone. And pacing. And sweating up a storm. All three symptoms likely caused by a giant, megasize case of wedding-day nerves.

Not out of doubt, Reid guessed, but from the enormity of what was about to occur. And he got that. Remembered that anxious state pretty damn clearly, as a matter of fact.

As Cole's best man, Reid figured it was his duty to bring him down a few levels. So he started off by saying, "Look at you, in that spiffy tux. One might think you're about to be married." He checked his watch. "Rather soon, at that."

"I might be ill, Reid," Cole said in complete seriousness. "Can't seem to settle my stomach or stop pacing." He walked to one end of the room and back again. "See? Can't stop."

Hiding his humor, Reid approached his brother and as Cole made another pass, grabbed him by the arms and guided him to a chair. "There, you've stopped, no thanks required. Maybe you should talk to me instead. You're not having second thoughts, are you?"

"No! God, no. I've been waiting for this day for what seems like forever." Rubbing his hand over his forehead, Cole scowled. "I don't know why I'm nervous. I shouldn't be nervous. There isn't another woman I can envision spending the rest of my life with."

"Normal to be nervous, Cole." Reid poured his brother a glass of water from the pitcher their mother had brought in earlier. "Drink this. Since you're not having second thoughts, I'd say these nerves have nothing to do with Rachel. They're about…the step and all that awaits."

Cole gulped half the water down in one fell swoop. "Right. That's a good thing."

"It is, trust me. And while I can't swear to this," Reid said, "as I never experienced the moment firsthand, I'm thinking your nerves—every last one of them—will disappear the second Rachel takes her first step down the aisle toward you."

"She'll be beautiful. And, yeah, that's a positive image." Slamming his empty hand against his heart, Cole let out a long whoosh of air. "This feels an awful lot like when I was still on the professional skiing circuit. Right before a competition, I'd get this pumped-up, crazy exhilaration along with…yeah, this woozy slide of nausea and nerves."

That sounded about right to Reid. "Go with this for a second. How would you feel once you were at the top of the course, ready for the push-off?"

"The nerves would fade." Cole snapped his fingers. "And I'd just have that powerful exhilaration, the…anticipation and hope of how the next few minutes would go."

"Well, I think you can assume the same will happen

here, only instead of anticipating the next few minutes, you'll have an entire lifetime with the woman you love." A solid stab of jealousy struck Reid, smack-dab in the center of his chest. Not *of* Cole or Rachel, or even what they had, but all that awaited them. "You're a lucky man."

"I am." Happiness glittered in Cole's gaze. "I love her, Reid. So damn much it shocks me at times. Like we'll be in the middle of a conversation, or she'll be sitting across the room from me, and all of a sudden, this bolt of awareness hits, and I'll almost keel over from the strength."

"I know how that is," he said quietly. "Treasure those moments, treasure Rachel, and…I don't know, man, never let any of this, any of what you two feel for each other, become commonplace. And…ah…I wouldn't mind a niece or nephew down the road."

That broke the ice. Cole laughed and stood, grabbed his jacket and slung it on. "Yes, Mom," he said. Pulling in a deep, centering breath, he turned toward Reid. "What about you? Are you doing okay? I mean, this is probably tough for you. Because of what happened and…"

"I'm fine. Today isn't about me," Reid said firmly, emphatically. "Today is about you and Rachel and celebration. Focus on that."

But Cole wasn't about to be dissuaded. "You're still holding to the wedding on May sixth? No thoughts on canceling or anything?"

"Nope." On this, Reid remained resolute. Scared to death most times, not that he would admit so to another soul, but resolute. "I love her, Cole." He winked and repeated his brother's words, saying, "So damn much it shocks me at times. And I guess I'm just not ready to let go."

"I wouldn't give up, either," Cole said after a brief, considering pause. "And you should know, I'll be there for you, if…well, if this doesn't go down the way it should. We'll… ah…go fishing or hiking or something. Just us."

"That sounds good. Real good." Emotion, far too soppy for Reid's comfort, roared in and clogged his throat. Family. Where would he be without it? Then, with a glance toward his watch, he said, "It's time. Let's go get you married, shall we?"

"Oh, hell," Cole said, every one of his nerves reappearing. "Really? It's time? Now?"

Laughing, Reid led his wobbly legged, nervous-as-all-get-out brother to the door, to the car, and then, into the church. And yup, once Rachel started her trek down the aisle, her eyes focused on Cole, Reid saw only happiness, excitement and pride in his brother's gaze.

That was an experience he'd like to have, seeing his bride—Daisy, of course—coming toward him with love in her eyes, and the rush of emotion such a sight would evoke.

Yeah, Reid thought again, his brother was one hell of a lucky man.

## Chapter Fourteen

Leaving Steamboat Springs was far more difficult than Daisy had anticipated. Partially because of the date—May fifth, a fact that struck her with no small amount of irony—and partially because everything that could have gone wrong on this day did.

Her parents had been continually delayed, and now they were set to arrive early that afternoon. Daisy wanted to be on the road by eight in the morning. Cowardly? Perhaps, but she saw no reason to put herself into an emotional spin before taking to the road for the long, fourteen-hour drive home. Besides which, Parker barely needed any help at this point.

Truthfully, she could have left a full week ago. She hadn't only because she'd enjoyed spending the time with her brother and the girls, and she wasn't entirely sure when she would be able to visit next. Well, Christmas for sure, but if possible, she'd like to make the trip sooner.

So, she'd awakened that Monday morning with a plan, and bit by bit, that plan fell to the wayside. First, she couldn't find her laptop. After close to an hour of searching, Erin had finally discovered it tucked in the linen closet, beneath a stack of towels. Parker said that Daisy had probably put it there accidentally, before her shower that morning, but…um…no.

Daisy did not tend to carry her laptop with her when her intentions were to stand in streaming hot water. Someone had hidden it, and initially, she'd thought one of the girls had done so in an attempt to keep her from leaving. They did not want her to go.

Neither admitted to the crime, and they were honest enough in their pleas that she began to wonder if the true culprit was her brother. Even so, she kept this thought to herself.

Then, after she'd completely packed her belongings and put her suitcases in her car, she was having a final cup of coffee with Parker. He stood, tripped, and her shirt was suddenly soaked clean through, requiring her to retrieve one of her bags and find a change of clothes.

Naturally, this solidified her belief that her brother was, for some unknown reason, trying to hamper her planned departure. She, again, decided to keep this to herself. Why leave on a sour note? But when her purse, with her car keys inside, also went missing, she'd had enough.

"What's going on here?" she asked Parker, her hands on her hips. "Because I know darn well where I left my purse, and now it's mysteriously vanished. Just like my laptop earlier."

Blue eyes blinked in feigned—she was sure—innocence. "I don't know, Daisy. Have you checked upstairs? Or maybe you stuck it in the trunk with your luggage? Or…" Pausing, he scratched his jaw and shrugged. "No clue. But we'll help you look."

The girls were home from school, due to a teacher in-service day, and they were more than willing to search the house. Another full hour of frustrated impatience passed before Daisy's purse was located by Megan. Under the kitchen sink, behind the extra-large bottle of dishwasher detergent and pretty much completely hidden from view.

And when the purse was found, Daisy saw her brother frown. What in heaven's name was he up to? She didn't know, but she planned on finding out. Posthaste.

"Hey, girls?" she said to Erin and Megan. "Can you take Jinx out in the backyard and play with her a bit, since she'll be stuck in the car all day? It would help me out a lot."

"We can do that, Aunt Daisy!" Megan said. "And we'll get her really tired, so she sleeps in the car and doesn't get scared."

"Since we won't be with her anymore," Erin added. "And she's used to us now."

"That would be perfect," Daisy said, knowing she was going to face a battle of emotions soon enough. Hers and her nieces. No, leaving them was not going to be easy. In any way.

The minute the girls were out of the house, she once again faced her brother. "I don't know what you're trying to do, but, Parker, I need to go home."

"Why?" he asked, settling himself on the living room sofa. His movements were slow and somewhat jerky, so it took him a minute to find a comfortable position. "I don't see why you can't stay for a few more days, or a week. Mom and Dad will be here. We haven't all been together since... well, since before you left the last time."

"I'm not ready for that, Parker," she said. "Mom alone, maybe. But Dad? He barely talks to me when I call to wish him happy birthday. I... No, I don't see how a face-to-face on the same day I'm leaving will do any good."

"Understandable. I just miss us all being a family, and with my accident—"

"We were never 'all' a family," she said tiredly. "You were, with Mom and Dad, and I was with you and Mom, but all four of us?" Daisy shook her head. "We weren't,

Parker. You know that as well as I do, and I don't believe you really expect that to change."

"Expect? Maybe not," he admitted, his voice low. "But I can hope, can't I? And Dad asks about you, Daisy. How you're doing, if I know if you're happy or dating anyone. I think he just doesn't know how to make that first move. So maybe if you were here…maybe that could change. It's worth a shot, isn't it? What's one more day?"

"You're such a great father, and I'm guessing a lot of who you are as a dad comes from our father, but, Parker," she said, trying to keep her emotions tightly in check, "I did not have that experience with him."

"Right. I know that, but come on. One. More. Day."

And she knew, in the snap of a finger, what was really going on. Tomorrow. The wedding. "This is more about Reid than Mom and Dad," she said, forming the statement as fact and not a question. "Why can't you let this go?"

"Because he loves you. And I've been living with you for the past few weeks, so it's fairly obvious that you love him, too."

"Sometimes," she said, "love isn't enough."

"That's cowardice speaking or…fear, maybe. Just go see him, Daisy. He has it in his head that he's pushed you too hard, so he's waiting, hoping you'll…just go see him."

She breathed in, deeply. Yes, Reid had pulled back significantly. He'd told her the same, that whatever happened, no matter what that was, remained in her hands. And that was good. Relieving. Empowering, too.

But she was still too afraid to take that damn step.

And she'd explained all of this to Parker in their many and extensive conversations on this topic. He'd made his stance very, very clear. And she'd done the same with hers. Simply speaking, she just did not have the energy to go into all of it again. Not with him. Heck, not even in her own head.

"I'm so happy you and I are becoming close." She went to him, sat next to him and rested her head on her big brother's shoulder. "And I will be here much more often. I love you, Parker. But part of this relationship means respecting each other's choices. And I can't stay."

Bringing his arm around her shoulders, he pulled her into a semi-awkward hug. "I love you, too, and okay," he said with a resigned sigh, "I'll respect your decision. Even if this particular one is…dead wrong." His fingers found her necklace and he gave it a gentle tug. "You're still wearing his ring, Daisy."

"Only because he refuses to take it back, and I don't want to lose it." Well, not the full truth. Close enough, though. Daisy stood and smoothed her hands down the front of her jeans. She wasn't wrong about this, about her decision. Couldn't be wrong. Not when so much was at stake. "Now, though, I need to get moving."

Goodbyes were said. Erin and Megan didn't cry, but when Daisy hugged each of them, they held on, their arms tight around Daisy's neck, for considerably longer than necessary. And no, part of her did not want to get in her car and drive away.

She'd done something important here. She'd built a connection with her nieces, her brother, and leaving felt odd and lonely and…sad. Incredibly, unbelievably sad.

But this, returning home, also held the lure of safety and comfort and stability. Three things she hadn't felt since her all-day date with Reid. She needed the comfort of home—*her* home—to find whatever peace of mind she'd lost. And, while she didn't quite comprehend the potency of the compulsion, her instincts were insistent that it was time.

That she had to go home, and she had to go home *now.*

"Okay, girls, listen up," she said, kneeling in front of them in the grass beside her car. "After I leave…if you go upstairs to your bedroom and look on your shelf, you'll find a present for each of you. Something special. And I hope that whenever you look at these gifts, you'll always remember how very, very much I love you."

For Erin, she'd purchased a small heart-shaped gold locket that contained two pictures, one of Bridget, Parker and the girls, and one of her and Jinx. With Erin's on-again, off-again need to have something to hug, she thought—hoped—the necklace would fill that requirement.

An idea she'd gotten from her own necklace and her recent propensity toward...well, hanging on to Reid's ring for dear life. The feel of that ring in her palm had given her comfort. She hoped the same would happen for Erin with the locket.

And for Megan, due to her color days, Daisy had bought a small charm bracelet. The band could be switched out for one of six colors, and the charms consisted of a locket with the same photos as Erin's. A miniature family, a dog, a pancake—yes, she'd actually found a pancake charm—a tiny doll and a few other mementos that she hoped would help Megan feel good, no matter the day's color.

Parker understood the reasoning behind both gifts, so he could explain that to the girls. And, she hoped by giving them something to focus on after she left, they'd be less sad.

"Thank you for the present, Aunt Daisy," Erin said in her oh-so-polite voice. "But I think I'd like it more if you stayed and just told us you loved us every day."

Megan dipped her chin in a definitive nod. "I think that, too. Please, please stay?"

Oh, Lord. She looked to Parker, but all he did was arch his brows and mouth the phrase, "One more day." Stricken with grief, with the acute sadness of two little girls she loved, she held out her arms, and said, "I'm sorry, but I really can't. Now come here for one more hug."

They piled in and she squeezed them as tight as she could, breathed in their scents and kissed them on their foreheads. One last hug with Parker while the girls fawned over Jinx, and that was that. Shortly after eleven, a good three hours later than her original plan, Daisy and Jinx were finally in the car, starting the long trip home.

And for the most part, Daisy felt…if not *good,* settled in her decision.

Jinx started whining about thirty miles out, a state of unhappiness that only increased the farther and longer Daisy drove. She pulled over several times for short walks and to give Jinx some extra attention, but none of that seemed to do the trick. All indications seemed to state—thankfully— that her dog wasn't ill. She just wasn't happy.

So Daisy talked with her as they drove. Tried to reassure her that everything was fine, that they were just going home. This calmed her for a little while, so Daisy continued with her constant stream of chatter. Well, about six hours into the trip, her murmuring words of comfort no longer had any effect, and Jinx's whining returned.

The eight-hour mark brought forth frantic whimpers, and ten hours in, Jinx began adding sharp, growling barks here and there between her whimpers and whines. At this point, all Daisy wanted was to get them home, so rather than stopping at a hotel, she pushed onward.

With less than two hours until they arrived at Daisy's apartment, Jinx's whimpers and whines dropped several levels in volume, and she curled up on the backseat. She did not fall asleep, but she quieted enough that Daisy could, finally, think.

About her departure from Steamboat Springs. About the looks on her nieces' faces as she drove off. About her conversation with her brother, and that her parents were now in the house that Daisy had considered her home since late February. And yes, she thought about Reid.

One by one, memories clicked into place, from their initial confrontation all the way through to their last. Every word, every look, every time he'd irritated her and every time he'd made her laugh. How he had somehow gotten through Jinx's defenses, and the absolute love he knew how to give—to Erin and Megan, to his family, to…Daisy.

All of it was there, available for her to consider, decipher, consider again and…at the end, revel in. As she did, a weight seemed to land on her chest, growing heavier as the miles went by, as she drew closer and closer to home. A desperate, almost clawing sensation began in her lower stomach, and by the time she pulled in to her apartment building's parking lot, she had gone straight from melancholy and confused to downright nauseous from emotion, from doubt.

In herself. In her decision.

Daisy parked her car and turned off the ignition. Closed her eyes and breathed deeply in an attempt to center herself. She was tired from the trip. Her head ached from the hours of Jinx's whining, whimpering and barking. Of course, she would be emotional.

Of course, she would have doubts.

Normal. Expected, even. She'd get a good night's sleep—in her own bed, thank goodness—and tomorrow all would seem better. Yawning, she clipped Jinx's leash to her collar for a quick walk before they went inside, and headed for the small dog park at the back of the building. The area was well-lit, the path easy to navigate, and as they walked, her dog continued to make soft, growly noises of unhappiness.

"Silly dog," Daisy said, unlatching the gate to the dog park. "We're home now."

Jinx gave her a look—a very human type of look—that seemed to state she couldn't believe Daisy had made such a ridiculous statement.

"Stop looking at me like that," Daisy said. "*This* is our home. Not Steamboat Springs."

With a snooty-sounding sniff, the whippet went to do her thing, and Daisy leaned against the fence to wait. The odd thought that this *wasn't* home crept into her consciousness, took root and expanded in size, increasing the sick jolt of nausea in her stomach.

As if in slow motion, Daisy pivoted to look at her apartment building. Three years she'd lived here. Three years this had been her home. And was, in fact, *still* her home.

But being here felt off. Wrong. And that strange, potent compulsion from earlier hadn't evaporated. The pull she'd ascribed toward needing to return home *now* was, if anything, stronger, more insistent, and…and…not about her physical residence.

Because this city, this building, no longer felt like home. *Reid.* Oh, Lord. What had she done?

Her legs weakened to the point that she sat down on one of the benches. Again, every moment she'd spent with Reid flickered to life in her head. He believed in her. He knew her, better perhaps, than she knew herself. And he still wanted her, still loved her, still believed they belonged together, and she…had run from him, from all of that, for the second damn time. *She'd* absconded from their team, even when he'd stood strong.

All at once, every tear she hadn't been able to shed in the past weeks came to be in a flood of emotion. But these tears were different in that they also came from a place of certainty. Every one of her fears now seemed ludicrous. Who cared how wide, how deep, how treacherous the leap was if, at the other end, she was with the man she loved.

The man who loved her.

Her doubts, one by one, disappeared. Because she understood, finally, that she did not have to take that leap alone. Reid would hold her hand and jump with her, and together they would not fall, they would…fly.

"Jinx!" Daisy said, unwilling to waste another second.

"We have to go, sweets. I…I have a wedding to get to. And barely enough hours to get there on time."

Her dog huffed and padded toward her, again with a very human type of look on her canine face. Something along the lines of "Duh. Took you long enough."

And then, without any sleep but with a blessedly happy and quiet dog, Daisy started the long journey back to Steamboat Springs, toward her real home. Toward Reid.

## Chapter Fifteen

On the afternoon of May sixth, surrounded by his family and a group of his closest friends, Reid waited to see if his faith would be rewarded. Via Parker, he knew that Daisy had, indeed, gotten in her car late yesterday morning to return to California.

She hadn't phoned Parker since, and out of concern, he'd attempted to get a hold of her, to no avail. He'd mentioned her phone had gone directly to voice mail, so Reid was holding on to one last slender thread of hope. Perhaps, he'd told Parker, she'd changed her mind somewhere along her route, had turned around and her cell's battery had died.

He wasn't a fool. It was just as possible, if not more so, that she had shut off her phone in order to completely retreat behind her turtle-porcupine shell. But any strand of hope was better than none, so until he had no other choice, he was holding on tight.

If she didn't show, if today did not pan out as he desperately wanted it to, then Reid had decided he'd give her some time—a month, tops—and he'd go to California. Hell. He'd pick up his life and move there, if she asked. But if she shot him down…well, he'd have to give up.

For her and for himself. And he'd be okay, eventually.

But at this moment, in this second, a chance still existed. So for now, he chose to focus on that, rather than worst-case scenarios.

Didn't mean he wasn't nervous, though.

Pulling in a breath, Reid smoothed his suit jacket, straightened his tie and appraised the space his mother had created. There were a multitude of flowers—wildflowers with silver brunia as a unifying element—in the corners, on the tables, adding bright splashes of color and fragrant scents of spring to the room. Some of the flowers had been used, along with twisted vines of greenery, to form an aisle for the bride to walk down.

Long, billowy sheaths of white, gauzy fabric were strung with twinkling lights in a mystical, almost fantastical display from the ceiling, softening the normally rustic appearance of the pub. And, finally, there were small, round lanterns in muted, soft shades on the bar and the tables that illuminated the entire area in a hazy, romantic glow.

Margaret Foster had outdone herself.

Daisy, Reid knew, would agree. And damn it, he wanted her to see this, wanted her to walk in here and spin in a circle, delighted by all she saw.

He glanced at the clock and immediately wished he hadn't. Fifteen minutes until what was supposed to be the start of their ceremony. His gut kicked in another blast of nerves, and his jaw ached from clenching it so hard. Purposefully, Reid relaxed his muscles, forced a smile and took a stroll around the room. People were chatting and watching the time, watching him, with concern and curiosity. Most were likely wondering how long it would take him to shut this thing down. Hell, he kept asking himself the same damn question.

When he reached the corner where his siblings stood, he stopped. "I'm fine," he said as way of greeting, before anyone could pose the question. "A little anxious, but fine.

And I figure, either way this goes, we can have one hell of a party. So no gloomy faces."

"She'll be here," Haley said, her eyes and her mouth firm and steady. "I believe she will be here, so…you believe that, too."

"We all hope she'll show," Dylan said, his voice low. "But have you determined how long you're going to wait?"

"As long as he wants." Cole frowned at Dylan. "There isn't a time limit on this, and," he said, now looking at Reid, "I'll stand here for however long that is."

Reid nodded, too choked up to form any actual words. Having the support of his brothers and sister meant the world. Fishing with Cole, he reminded himself, if this went sour. Just the two of them. That would be good.

Finding his voice again, he said, "I see Parker and the girls, his parents. Think I'll go say hi, see how they're all doing or if they need anything."

"Sure. But I'm guessing if he'd heard from Daisy, he'd not waste time telling you," Dylan said, accurately pegging Reid's motivation. Or, at least, part of his motivation. "We could go upstairs, have a drink and just hang loose there for a while."

Nice idea, and Reid was grateful for the thought, the offer. But if Daisy walked in those doors, he wanted to know it instantly. "Thanks, but…rather stay here. Think I'll be more nervous if I'm in any other room. Better to keep moving, talking."

So that was what he did. No, Parker had not heard from Daisy, and no, he had not yet been able to reach her. He spoke with his father and his mother, both of whom were just as calm and supportive as he needed them to be. But every time Reid looked at the clock, a chunk of minutes had disappeared. Now it was four forty-five, and…well, much as he hated to admit it, he was beginning to lose what remained of his hope, his belief.

She had to show. He *knew* they belonged together.

By five-fifteen, he decided he'd hold off on the no-wedding announcement for one more hour. Longer, probably, than he should wait, but he kept thinking…couldn't get it out of his head, that if Daisy had driven all the way home before changing her mind, there was no way she'd have been able to do the return trip and be here by four.

He checked with the minister, a friend of his father's, to make sure he could wait that long. He could, he said, no problem. So. Six-fifteen, no later than six-thirty was Reid's cutoff.

'Course, if she showed at midnight tonight, he'd be good with that, too. Really, he just wanted her here. With him. Whenever and however and—

He heard the bark first. That strange, not-a-growl, not-a-yowl, not-a-yip bark that could only come from one specific, ornery-as-all-get-out creature. *Jinx.* And he knew, thank God almighty, he knew that his belief, his hope, his faith had not been in vain.

Heart galloping like a herd of wild horses, legs loose and wobbly, Reid made the slow, slow pivot to face the door. And there she was, standing in the entrance with that dog, whom he also loved, in her arms, wearing a wedding dress that was…a bit rumpled but still gorgeous, flyaway hair and tired but frantic eyes. To Reid, Daisy had never looked so beautiful.

Because she was here, for him, for them, and he'd waited for this one moment in time for…well, eight years. To the friggin' day.

All of his strength reappeared. His heart calmed, his legs steadied and he strode across the room, wanting her in his arms, his lips on her lips, and if she agreed, her hand in his from this day forward, for better or for worse, in sickness and in health.

"Reid," she said, the second he was in hearing distance.

"I'm so sorry I wasn't here on time. So, so sorry. I tried. Broke every speed limit, which, okay, probably not the best idea on no sleep, and had to stop to put on the dress, but I did not want you standing here, waiting for me. I did not want to be late, so—"

"Marry me, darlin'?"

Eyelashes fluttered and joy entered her gaze, wiping out the anxious adrenaline he'd seen but a second ago. "Yes," she said, loudly. Clearly. "Yes, I will marry you."

Whistles and cheers and applause filled the room, along with Jinx's yips of...happiness? Sure as hell sounded like it to Reid. And, frankly, he was done pretending that this dog wasn't more human than canine when, clearly, she was.

Everything happened really fast then. Erin came forward to claim Jinx, while Haley and Rachel and his mother stole Daisy into the back, to help set her hair and such to straights. He didn't see the sense in that, as she truly had never looked more stunning.

And then, amidst the flowers and the lanterns and the gauzy, romantic fabric, with his family and hers in attendance, the Lennox-Foster wedding, eight years after their original intent, finally commenced, and Daisy became his wife.

"Daisy Foster," he said with a grin and a wink. "May I kiss you now?"

He didn't wait for a response, sort of figuring that marriage superseded rule number two, and just gathered her close and lowered his mouth. When their lips met, a feeling of pure, perfect rightness settled in, filling him with a deep and satisfying sense of wholeness. This connection, the potency and power that existed between them, was intrinsic. Natural.

And sexy as hell.

Desire, hot and strong and alive, shot through him and raised his pulse, heated his blood. Never had any other woman had this effect on him. Never *could* another woman reach his body, his heart and his soul with such point-blank accuracy or completeness.

She was his. He was hers.

And he would protect her, love her, for the rest of his life.

Remembering they had an audience, he broke the kiss. "I love you, Daisy," he whispered. "Then and now. Still and forever. And I will never let you doubt that again."

"I have no more doubts, Reid. Not about us," she said, her eyes a tantalizing shade of green. "And I promise you that the only running I'll do from here on out is toward you."

"Aw, darlin', it's good to hear you say that, but," he said, unable to stop himself, "I'd like to remind you that I was right in this matter. I told you that I believed you'd change your mind, that you'd be here for this wedding. And it looks as if—"

That was all he got out before she kissed him.

# *Epilogue*

"Hold still, you crazy dog," Daisy said to Jinx, who was hopping around as if she were a bunny rabbit. "I know you want to go outside and play with Reid and the girls, but we have to take care of this one little surprise first. Please?"

Quickly, before Jinx took off, she attached the small, gift-size envelope to her dog's collar, in the exact same fashion Reid had slightly over a year ago. Once the envelope was secure and Jinx's collar wasn't too loose, she led the dog to the back door.

"Okay, you know what to do," she said, opening the door. "Take that to Reid, sweets."

Off Jinx went, roaring through the grass to join Reid, Parker and the girls in their game of Frisbee. Smiling, beyond happy, Daisy placed her hand on her stomach and watched, hoping her husband would notice the envelope sooner rather than later.

She couldn't wait to share her news. They were having a baby. In December.

And she'd decided to tell him via a "We're Having a Baby!" card, similar to all of those frustrating save-a-date cards he'd left lying around Parker's house for her to find.

Seemed appropriate. And fun.

In the thirteen months since their wedding, she hadn't experienced a single regret in her emotional rush of a decision to turn around and return to Steamboat Springs. Life was good. About as perfect as a person could hope for, actually. She was madly in love.

Then and now. Still and forever.

All of her relationships were strong, or becoming stronger. She and her brother were rock-solid, and she adored her nieces with a wholehearted joy that continued to grow. The well of love she had for them seemed never ending.

She'd even, slowly and carefully, started mending the rift with her parents. Easier with her mother. Clara Lennox had profusely expressed her regrets, her apologies, and Daisy had accepted and forgiven. They were almost as close as they once had been, and for that, Daisy was grateful. Having her mother in her life again was a gift.

And her father...well, that would take more time, more caution, but she believed they were on the right road to becoming closer. Charles Lennox had apologized, as well. He'd even stated that his struggle in accepting Daisy was unfair, and that he hadn't realized how much he'd considered her his daughter until she was gone.

Would they ever have the type of relationship she'd once dreamed of? Probably not. Love existed between them, though, and she believed—or hoped—that given time, that love could help them form a nurturing, positive father-daughter relationship. As Reid liked to say, hope existed, and where there was hope, any damn thing on the face of the earth could happen.

So she chose to hope.

A series of barks pulled her from her thoughts, and her smile widened. In delight and in heady anticipation. Reid was almost sprinting toward the back door, with Jinx in excited pursuit.

Obviously, he'd found and read her card.

In less than twenty seconds, he was standing in front of her, his dark eyes intent, searching. Already concerned, she guessed, along with thrilled.

"A baby?" he asked, his voice holding every ounce of that concern, that thrill. "You're sure? No doubts on this in any way?"

"Hmm? Oh, the baby?" she said. "Absolutely positive. You're going to be a father sometime in December. Isn't that—"

"December? In the middle of the winter season, when I'm hardly ever here?" His concern grew, and she almost—*almost*—laughed. "So from early November on, you'll have to spend more time with my family. Or your brother, because I don't want you alone, and—"

"Maybe even a Christmas baby...wouldn't that be something?"

"We'll have to work out a system, so someone is with you when I'm not around. Dylan. He'd be a good choice." Reid closed his eyes and Daisy could just about see the wheels turning. "Parker, of course, but with the girls...no. Will have to be Dylan. Maybe he can even move in for the duration, or maybe your mom—"

And, as she had done at their wedding and many, many times since then, she walked up to her sexy, loving, protective husband, put her hands on his shoulders and kissed him.

Fully. Soundly.

He shut up and kissed her back. Also fully. Also soundly.

It was, she decided, the perfect arrangement.

\* \* \* \* \*

## *A sneaky peek at next month…*

# Cherish™

**ROMANCE TO MELT THE HEART EVERY TIME**

## *My wish list for next month's titles…*

**In stores from 17th January 2014:**

☐ Daring to Trust the Boss – Susan Meier

& Heiress on the Run – Sophie Pembroke

☐ A Sweetheart for Jude Fortune – Cindy Kirk

& Celebration's Bride – Nancy Robards Thompson

**In stores from 7th February 2014:**

☐ Rescued by the Millionaire – Cara Colter

& Moonlight in Paris – Pamela Hearon

☐ The Summer They Never Forgot – Kandy Shepherd

& His Forever Girl – Liz Talley

Available at WHSmith, Tesco, Asda, Eason, Amazon and Apple

## *Just can't wait?*